"The woods give us plenty of places to hide."

"Come. I found a place where you can get a little sleep." Nick helped Kristen to her feet. "I'll be close enough to hear you if you have trouble, but far enough away to give you privacy."

So considerate, so thoughtful that she might need some time alone.

As if she needed to think about Nick Sandoval's benefits. "I'm sorry I dragged you into this."

"I think I'm the one who dived into this."

She smiled. "I should have listened and not gone off on my own."

"It's done, Kristen. You can't undo the past. You can only move on with the future." He laughed, though she didn't know why. "Try to sleep."

She couldn't deny his kindness.

Or the fact that her feelings for him weren't exactly brotherly.

She smiled and dreamed of a Fourth of July celebration with fireworks shooting brilliant stars and flowers and flags into the air.

And awoke gasping for breath with the realization the fireworks of her dream were, in wakeful reality, gunshots.

Laurie Alice Eakes dreamed of being a writer from the time she was a small child. Now, with her dreams fulfilled, she is the award-winning and bestselling author of over two dozen historical and contemporary novels. When she isn't writing full-time, she enjoys long walks, live theater and being near her beloved Lake Michigan. She lives in Illinois with her husband and sundry cats and dogs.

Books by Laurie Alice Eakes

Love Inspired Suspense

Perilous Christmas Reunion
Lethal Ransom

LETHAL RANSOM
LAURIE ALICE EAKES

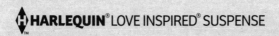

HARLEQUIN® LOVE INSPIRED® SUSPENSE

Recycling programs
for this product may
not exist in your area.

LOVE INSPIRED BOOKS

ISBN-13: 978-1-335-67890-4

Lethal Ransom

www.Harlequin.com

Printed in U.S.A.

There is no fear in love; but perfect love casteth out fear: because fear hath torment. He that feareth is not made perfect in love.
−1 John 4:18

To Red, whose friendship encouraged me through this difficult year and helped keep me writing.

ONE

Kristen Lang had to be mistaken. The same vehicle that had followed her from her office to the courthouse where she'd picked up her mother, the Honorable Julia Lang, could not be tailing her down the Eisenhower out of Chicago. The world was surely full of gunmetal-gray SUVs.

With her mother's job, threats were not uncommon. For the past ten years of her life, Kristen had learned to be vigilant of anything out of the ordinary.

Seeing the same—or very similar—vehicle three times in one afternoon was out of the ordinary.

Kristen took one second to glance at her mother. "Is everything all right with you?"

"When is it not?" Mom's voice sounded a little too bright.

"Oh, I don't know, Mom. Maybe when someone threatened to blow up your car, or you had that stalker two years ago, or—"

"Why would you think anything is wrong now?"

"Because you're not answering my question with anything but questions." Kristen checked her rearview mirror.

The dark SUV loomed closer.

Beside her, Mom sighed. "I have no reason to think anything is wrong. I haven't had any threatening phone calls or mail."

"But?" Kristen squeezed the word past the tightening of her chest.

"Nothing that doesn't make me sound like a silly old woman."

Kristen laughed at that. "You are the last person I would call silly or old."

"Thank you for protecting my ego." Her mom patted Kristen's hand on the steering wheel. "Now tell me what's going on with you."

Defeated for the moment, Kristen shrugged. "Everyone else left the office early for one reason or another, and I decided to finish up paperwork at home. You know I don't like being there alone."

"I don't blame you. If you had an office in a better part of town, that wouldn't be a problem."

"We're there to be closer to our clients."

"If you had better clients, such as ones who pay—"

"Someone has to advocate for poor victims of crimes. And I get paid, Mom, you know that."

"A tenth what you would make if you'd gone to law school."

Kristen sighed over the age-old conversation. "I wouldn't be doing as much good as I am now for those who can't afford to pay to get help."

The work she was certain God wanted her to do, but her mother didn't want to hear that.

"You could do pro bono work with better support staff than you get at that nonprofit organization you work for now."

With the rain starting to fall more heavily, Kristen concentrated on her driving and didn't answer. Rain made the road slick, and her tires weren't the best. One moment of inattention, one need to slam on the brakes, and they could hydroplane into the path of a larger vehicle like a truck.

Or an SUV appearing out of nowhere again.

She shivered, and her knuckles whitened on the steering wheel.

"It's not too late to change your career." Mom's voice broke her concentration. "You're only twenty-five. It's too late to get into a law school this year, but if you apply this fall, you can start next year. You'll only be twenty-nine when you finish."

Kristen didn't want the sort of corporate lawyer job her mother thought good enough. She liked being a social worker, helping rebuild people's lives.

"I thought you wanted me to get married." Hearing the sarcasm in her voice, she opened her mouth to apologize.

"I would, of course, but you don't seem to meet any men on your own or like any of the men I introduce you to," Mom said first. "I saw Marcus Ashburton today, and he said you turned him down for a second date. Why?"

"He's boring."

Traffic was anything but boring, especially with that SUV behind her. Kristen wanted to concentrate on driving, not discuss her love life—or lack thereof—with her mother, the matchmaker.

"That young lawyer you went out with last week is a good man," Mom continued. "He does a great deal of pro bono work."

Kristen grimaced. Marcus had spent nearly the entire dinner talking about his "charity" work and how good a person it made him. Not a way into Kristen's good graces. If someone had to tell her he was good, he was probably drawing attention away from too many parts of him that were not.

"He says he's good."

At being nice, at being a lawyer, at choosing fine restaurants. He probably thought he sneezed better than anyone else.

"I don't like him," Kristen said. "He only does the sort of free legal services that bring him maximum attention from the press."

Kristen struggled to keep one eye on the dark SUV bobbing in and out of her rearview mirror, and the other eye on traffic. The latter seemed to close in on her so much she could scarcely breathe. And the former was drawing near.

"The press loves him."

Even if she hadn't found him boring, she'd never date a man with a job that kept him so busy—a man she couldn't count on to be home when she needed him. Her lawyer father had been absent for nearly every important moment in her life.

"I don't want to talk about Marcus, Mom." Kristen sounded tenser than she intended.

"All right, but I was sure you would like him."

"He's a perfect gentleman. He's just not my type."

Mom pulled her phone from her bag and

began to text. "What is your type?" she asked as her thumbs flew across the screen keyboard.

"Someone who...um..."

She forgot the question she was answering as the dark SUV filled her rearview mirror.

She needed to get away from that vehicle, return to the left lane. If she could find an opening in the line of cars and trucks streaming past her, she would accept traveling beside the "L" train. Anything to get clear of that behemoth riding too close to her rear bumper.

"See, you don't even know what you want." Mom sounded victorious.

Mom's phone pinged with an incoming text, so Kristen didn't bother to respond. Her goal required her attention. She needed an opening.

Nothing but endless vehicles sending up plumes of rain water. Nothing... Nothing...

Yes. There! A break in traffic at last.

She stomped on the gas in an attempt to surge into the break in traffic. Zero to sixty in her aging vehicle was more like zero to thirty, but she managed to slip into the next lane.

And that oversize SUV cut in right behind her, its engine far more powerful than hers.

Kristen wanted to scream in frustration and beat the steering wheel instead of gripping it like a rip cord on a parachute jump.

If only she could bail—from the highway,

from the conversation with her mother, from the fear that the vehicle was following them, or more likely her mother, the judge who often made unpopular decisions in the name of justice and had experienced trouble in the past.

And this time, the second time since Kristen was fifteen, the pursuer was bringing her into the picture.

Unless she was mistaken and this wasn't the same vehicle. That was entirely possible. Likely, even. Only, past events were making her anxious.

"You don't even know which lane you want to drive in." Mom didn't raise her gaze from the phone in her hands. "And you're going too fast for the conditions."

"I'm trying to keep up with traffic so we're not run over by that monster behind us."

"You're too close to the car ahead of us."

She was, but only by a car length or so. If she dropped back, that SUV would be too close by about a gazillion feet.

"Kristen, get back into the right lane."

"How? I forgot my shoehorn."

"Don't be sarcastic. It isn't attractive."

Kristen sighed. Her mother—every carefully blond hair, dyed to look natural, lay in place in an elegant twist, her makeup glowed as fresh as it had been that morning, and her charcoal-gray suit hung on her slim frame without a wrinkle—might be a circuit judge in the federal court system, but she was still a mother and applied herself to the role with as much vigor as she had applied herself to everything else in her life.

"There's an opening coming up where you can get back into the right lane." Mom tapped on the side window.

Kristen shook her head. "Can't make it."

"If you had a better car—"

"Please, don't start."

She was too tired and too worried about that gunmetal-gray SUV to deal with the "If you had a better job, you could have a better car" lecture. At that moment, she needed to tell her Mom she intended to get off at the next Oak Park exit instead of continuing to her mother's house farther west. She needed to lose this tail before she led him straight to her mother's home—or her own.

But the SUV was even closer.

"Kristen," Mom said with exaggerated patience, "get into the right lane. You can move in there."

"But I want to exit the expressway."

"Not here."

"Who's driving here?" Kristen tried to laugh to lighten the question.

"Just listen to me for once."

Kristen glanced at her mother and read tension in the tightening of the skin around her blue eyes.

"You know," Kristen murmured.

"That we're being followed? Yes. Now change lanes."

Hands gripping the steering wheel hard enough for her knuckles to whiten, Kristen managed to slide into the slower lane.

And the dark SUV wedged in right behind her. Mere inches from her bumper. Just as her foot pressed harder on the gas to create more distance between her Camry and the SUV, a pickup roared into the gap between Kristen and the car ahead of her.

"What are they doing?" Kristen cried.

Mom didn't answer. She held her phone to her ear. "I think we are about to be carjacked."

"Mom, who are you talking to?" Kristen's voice had gone squeaky again as she sought for breath—breath and the Harlem Avenue exit. She passed it every day, and she couldn't remember if it was on the left or the right. She couldn't remember if Austin or Harlem was first.

Her sweating palms slipped on the steering wheel, and the car swerved. "I need to get off the expressway."

"We're easier to find if we stay on the Eisenhower." Mom's tone remained quiet, calm. "If we get off in Oak Park, there's too many quiet side streets we could end up on."

And the exit loomed too close. Moving over for a left-hand exit was impossible at the moment. The pickup was slowing. The SUV was not. The faster lane flowed with an unbroken line of cars and trucks. At the moment, a semi roared alongside them, flinging water from beneath its enormous tires, sending diesel fumes into the intake vents for the air-conditioning.

Kristen's stomach rolled with the anticipation of what was about to happen and the knowledge she might fail at the drastic measure she must take in an attempt to stop it.

"Mom?" Kristen kept her tone as calm as she could manage. "Hold on."

She spun the wheel to the right.

"Don't do it," Mom cried.

Too late. The Camry's tires rumbled on the edge of the pavement. The car hit the shoulder, water and rocks spraying, pinging against the fenders. Kristen's foot pressed harder on the gas. Fifty-five. Sixty. Sixty-five.

"Kristen!" Mom shouted.

She saw it looming in her rearview mirror— the SUV riding her bumper. Ahead, a disabled vehicle stood on the side of the highway, flashers blazing into the rain-created twilight. To her left, the pickup kept pace, blocking her ability to swing back into the flow of traffic.

Trapped, she eased up on the gas, praying the SUV wouldn't crash into them, and moved her foot to the brake. Slow and steady. Water flooded over the road. She could hydroplane and cause a pileup if she slammed on the brakes and lost control. If she didn't stop fast enough, she would plow into the aged Buick ahead of her.

She was losing momentum too quickly. The back of the Camry fishtailed. The SUV blasted its horn, and Kristen jumped.

"Just past the Harlem exit," Mom was saying into her phone.

"Put the phone down." Kristen barked out the order. "If we crash, it could break your face."

If they crashed? When they crashed.

Or something crashed into them.

The thud came from the left, a tap against the bumper. From the corner of her eye, she caught sight of the SUV looming dark and menacing in her side mirror. Roaring up closer, crowding her to the right where she could go over no farther. Threatening the back of the pickup.

Bang.

The SUV hit the left-hand back door. Kristen's foot slammed on the brake in a convulsive effort to maintain control. Water blasted against the undercarriage.

And control was only a dream.

The Camry spun perpendicular to the lane, missed the pickup by a hair, then smashed its front bumper into the side of the SUV.

The air bags exploded, slamming Kristen against her seat, driving wind from her lungs. Mom emitted a soft gasp, then began to cough from the dust.

Kristen couldn't breathe at all. Her vision blurred. Her chest tightened, squeezing, squeezing...

Between the air bag and seat belt, she couldn't move. Cocooned. Strangled. The air bag was already deflating. A click and the seat belt would be off. This was mere seconds.

It felt like a lifetime.

A scream reverberated through her head, couldn't reach her lips, choked her.

"No panic attacks now." Mom never raised her voice, but it was sharp nonetheless. "No weakness."

Weakness. Mom considered panic attacks weakness. Must not show weakness.

Nausea clawed at Kristen's middle. She swallowed, reached for the seat belt lock with one hand and the door handle with the other.

The door popped open without her aid. It

should have been locked, but a man stood in the opening on her side and another on Mom's side.

"Get out," the man on the right commanded.

"Stupid move there, lady," the man on Kristen's side said. "Who taught you to drive?"

"I will wait for the police here in the vehicle." Mom made the declaration and folded her hands against her waist.

"You're going to get out now." The man on her side grabbed her arm and reached across to release her seat belt.

Mom moved her hands to the dashboard. "I do not wish to go into the rain."

"Even if your car explodes?" The man on Kristen's side grabbed her arm and began to haul her from the car.

She slammed her fist against his wrist. The move failed on a full-grown man. He continued to hold. She grabbed for the steering wheel, curled her fingers around the grip.

With a squeeze of the man's hand on her wrist, her fingers opened against her will, freeing her hold on the wheel. And then he was dragging her into the rain, icy for June, painful for rain. Hail. Tiny hammer blows against her face. She ducked her head, saw her feet in their sensible pumps scraping along the pavement as though they belonged to someone else.

They may as well belong to someone else.

She possessed no power to stop herself from being forced from her car.

Carjacking was all too common. People stole cars to commit a crime, but they didn't usually hurt the vehicle owners. They left them beside the road. It was unpleasant but not life threatening if they didn't fight back.

But these men were taking her and her mother, not the car. They had deliberately wrecked her.

She yanked one arm free and struck out for the man's face. Missed. She kicked one kitten heel into the man's shin. Connected. He grunted, then picked her up and tossed her over his shoulder in a fireman's carry. Tires, a barely dented bumper on the SUV, wet pavement, Mom's designer heels spun past in a nauseating blur. In another moment, she was going to be sick.

The man tossed her into the back of the SUV. Her head hit the side. Stars exploded before her eyes. Dazed, she lay still for a fatal moment—a moment in which her mother landed beside her.

"Tie her up," one man commanded.

He leaned into the back of the SUV and grabbed Mom's hands.

Kristen surged up and bashed her head into his face at the same time Mom shoved both stilettos into his middle. He staggered back, fell against his companion, sending him reeling, but still held Mom's hands.

"Kristen, run!" her mom cried.

Kristen ran, kicking off her pumps and speeding along the shoulder of the Eisenhower. Above the roar of traffic, she heard the slam of the SUV's hatch—with her mother behind its tinted windows.

Traffic slowed to a crawl and Nick Sandoval knew he had found what he'd been looking for, what he'd feared he would find since receiving the phone call from his boss.

"Judge Lang contacted us to say she fears they're about to be carjacked." Callahan's voice was as calm as usual, but Nick knew the US marshal for the northern district of Illinois well enough to catch the tension beneath. "I've called the local law enforcement and am sending men out from here, but you're on your way in that direction, aren't you?"

"I am."

Despite all his responsibilities, Nick's boss remembered this was Monday night, the night Nick ate dinner with his eldest sister's family. Unlike Wednesday night when he joined his younger brother and sister-in-law, and Friday nights, when the entire clan gathered at their parents' house for Mom's great cooking and terrible attempts to get her last unmarried child to commit to someone—again—no matter how many times Nick told her he wasn't ready to put his fiancée's death behind him.

"She's in her daughter's car," Callahan continued with his deliberately slow explanation. "It's a silver Camry."

"That should be easy to spot. There must only be a hundred within a mile."

Despite his sardonic response, Nick's instincts for trouble tingled up his spine as his eyes fell on the slowed traffic ahead.

"Got to go, sir. Something up ahead." Still hearing his boss's voice squawking from the speaker, Nick tossed the phone onto the passenger seat. He needed both hands on the wheel, and his vintage Mustang didn't possess anything as fancy as a Bluetooth connection to the car speakers.

Sirens wailed in the distance, audible above the rain drumming on the Mustang's roof and roar of surrounding traffic. Cops were on their way, but Nick wanted to get to the scene first if it involved the judge. Protecting federal judges was his primary duty.

An accident involving the judge would be worse than a carjacking. Oddly enough, the latter were usually peaceful with drivers forced off the road, removed from their vehicles, left stranded while the crooks took off in the vehicle to commit a crime, such as a robbery or drive-by shooting, and then abandon the car, usually wrecked, somewhere else. In that scenario, the car might be a loss, but the judge and her daughter would be safe. Wet. Cold. Probably frightened, but unharmed.

His gaze swept the traffic and his mind touched on the idea that if this was a carjacking, it wasn't like those that went down in the city so often they rarely made the news anymore.

Maybe the traffic jam had nothing to do with Her Honor. Nick couldn't risk picking up his phone to call Callahan to ask if or what he had heard. Neither had the phone rung. A good sign, surely.

An opening in the right lane was another good sign. Nick punched the accelerator and surged into the gap seconds before everyone's brake lights flared on and the lane screeched to a complete halt—a defining characteristic of an accident, not a carjacking.

Unless…

Nick cut the wheel right and, half a dozen horns honking in his wake, plowed onto the shoulder of the road.

He spied what lay ahead now. An accident for sure. A crash between a dark gray SUV and a silver Camry, the former idling with emergency flashers engaged, the latter with doors wide-open.

And from the vehicles raced a tall woman in a flowing summer dress and long, blond hair, with a man in hot pursuit.

Nick flung himself from his car and raced for the woman. The daughter? Not the judge. Where was Her Honor? His gaze flicked to the Camry, to the SUV. Rescue the daughter? Go look for the judge? His duty was to the judge, but the daughter was in imminent danger.

Wishing he wore his running shoes, Nick sprinted along the side of the road. Cars honked. People shouted, words indistinct above the rumble of engines and approaching sirens. His feet slipped on wet gravel.

A hundred yards ahead of him, the woman stumbled, started to pitch forward. The man in pursuit grabbed a handful of her hair and jerked her upright. Her mouth opened. If she cried out, ambient noise drowned the sound.

Nick pushed himself to greater speed. The man was dragging the woman backward, closer to him. She struck out with one hand. The man caught her wrist, spun her around toward the idling SUV nosed against the Camry.

That SUV was involved in more than having wrecked the Camry. Nick knew it with all his law enforcement instincts for trouble. On foot, even in his Mustang, he couldn't stop the owners of the SUV if it took off. From its angle, he could read the license plate. Police were on their way but taking too long. Minutes when Nick needed seconds, wedged into traffic as he had been despite their sirens.

But he could stop that man from taking the judge's daughter. A dozen drivers and their passengers could stop the man from taking her. Not one person got out of their vehicle. Scared. The man could be armed. Nick was armed. Still, if anyone simply tossed something in the way to trip the man Nick would catch them before they reached that SUV.

"Seconds. I only need seconds to gain."

Half prayer, half plea to anyone who might be willing, Nick spoke the words aloud, though he barely heard them. Ten yards. Three yards.

Nick lunged and grasped the daughter's captor. "I'm a deputy US marshal. Let her go."

The man tried to keep running, hold firm on the judge's daughter. But she stopped, dropped to her knees, an anchor to her captor.

"Get up." The man aimed a kick in the young woman's direction.

Nick hooked the man's raised leg with his own foot and threw him off balance. "Now stay down." He placed his foot in the center of the man's chest. "If you can, get up and head for my car behind me."

"I can't. My mom—" She spoke between gasps for breath, then leaped up and began running toward the SUV.

"Stop," Nick shouted.

She kept running.

Nick's prisoner laughed and tried to grasp his ankle.

Nick grabbed the man's wrists and hauled him to his feet. "Who are you?"

"Who are *you*?" Four cops from the nearest suburban town surrounded Nick.

"Deputy US Marshal Nick Sandoval. Please take this man into custody. I need to go after the judge's daughter."

And the judge? Of course. The young woman was running toward her mother.

"Credentials?" the police sergeant demanded.

"Later." Nick thrust the prisoner, a man nearly half his size, toward the waiting police officers. "I'm responsible for those ladies."

An officer caught hold of the prisoner, and Nick raced after the judge's daughter. It took mere seconds to catch up with her—seconds in which the flashers on the SUV ceased, the tires spun, and the monstrous vehicle roared to life. One officer raised his weapon as though intending to shoot out the tires.

"No," Nick shouted, as another officer pushed his colleague's arm down.

They couldn't fire at a vehicle containing a federal judge. They could miss the tires and strike her through the rear of the vehicle. They could hit a tire and send the SUV spinning or rolling into the heavy traffic—traffic unable to stop because of the rain-slick road.

Two officers ran for their cruisers to give chase, but the SUV swept past the wrecked Camry and sped along a suddenly clear shoulder, pickup and stalled vehicles gone. Before the police reached their car, the SUV was lost in traffic.

"Nooo." The daughter's cry was long and painful like a wounded animal.

She took a few stumbling steps in the direction the SUV, then dropped to her knees, her hands to her cheeks.

"It's all right—" Nick hesitated, not sure of her name, as he crouched beside her. "You're safe with me."

"But they have my mother." She was gasping as though still running. "They took my mother."

"We'll find her. We caught the man who grabbed you. He'll tell us something."

Not at all guaranteed, but she needed reassurance.

"Let's get you to my car and out of the rain."

"We need to go after that SUV. They have my mom."

The judge, Nick's responsibility.

The minute he helped the woman to her feet and turned toward his vehicle, he knew her assailant had slipped the officers' custody. The officers were scattered, running into the now halted traffic, and the wiry kidnapper darted between cars and under the elevated train tracks to the eastbound lane.

No one would blame Nick for the vehicle getting away. He could not have caught up with it.

But they might blame him for the prisoner escaping.

TWO

Kristen fell more than sat in the deputy marshal's low-slung car and covered her face with her hands. She should lock the doors, make herself safe. But she couldn't in such a small space. Only the rain-washed air, however choked with exhaust fumes, kept her from hyperventilating.

Her feet throbbed from running barefoot along the highway. Her head ached from where the man had grabbed her by the hair. Her shoulder hurt from how he tried to drag her away until the deputy US marshal arrived to rescue her, too late for her mother.

She began to shake from the cold of being soaked through, from the accident and near capture, from knowing her mother was tossed into a car and speeding away somewhere. *Nightmare* seemed too tame a word to describe the events of the past fifteen minutes.

Her mother had been kidnapped, and her father was thousands of miles away, probably out of cell phone range.

With two parents who worked so much that nannies had raised their daughter more than them, Kristen understood feeling alone. But nothing, not all the school plays and choir concerts Mom or Dad or both of them had been unable to attend, left her as hollow as knowing men had taken her mother by force and she had been unable to stop them. On the contrary, her mother had stopped them from taking Kristen.

She slumped forward so her forehead rested on the dashboard. "If I had made different driving choices... If I had told a marshal at the courthouse about the SUV following me... If I thought faster during the accident—"

More police cars arrived. Blaring sirens ceased, though lights flashed in an eye-searing strobe behind her. The police were here, while her mother was somewhere else. She was here, while her mother was somewhere else. Her mother was in the hands of a criminal, while she would soon be in the hands of the police or US Marshals Service. Whoever it was would be questioning her like she was a suspect. They might send her a victim's advocate.

A bubble of hysterical laughter rose in her throat. After the hundreds of crime victims she had helped in her job as a social worker, she was now one herself. She should know exactly what to expect.

But she doubted anyone could prepare for such an eventuality. None of her training had taught her about the slicing depth of the guilt, the anguish, the grief of being captured even for a few minutes.

And her mother could be captured for hours or days, or—

She wouldn't think about the worst-case scenario.

A groan escaped Kristen's lips. "Mom, why do you stay in this job?"

Threats had been nothing before, but that didn't mean someone wouldn't end up following through. Except Mom hadn't mentioned any threats. Surely she wouldn't keep such information from the marshals who were assigned to protect the judges, even if she might keep it from her daughter.

And her husband?

Kristen should have asked, would have, if she hadn't been so wrapped up in looking for that SUV—the vehicle now speeding away with her mother inside alone because she had helped Kristen escape.

Sick with guilt, Kristen reached for the marshal's phone. Her own remained in her purse in her car a quarter mile ahead on the side of the road. Abandoned. Wrecked.

"Siri, call—" Kristen stopped. She couldn't remember her father's number. She didn't know her mother's number. She never bothered to remember telephone numbers anymore. They were programmed into her phone.

She needed it—now.

She slid out of the sports car and took a step toward her bashed-in car. Gravel cut into her feet, and she cried out in pain. It was foolish to have kicked off her shoes to run faster.

She had run away while that man stole her mother.

Every time she turned around, she was disappointing her mother. She wouldn't take the right sort of job. She wouldn't drive a better car. She wouldn't date the right class of men. Kristen was happier at home with a good movie and a bowl of popcorn than she was at a black-tie affair or any sort of gathering where people's worth seemed to be measured in the cost of their ensembles rather than their character.

Letting her mother get kidnapped was one more huge disappointment, one more misstep to letting her parent down.

"If she dies, it'll be my fault." Kristen wiped her eyes.

This was no time to give in to tears or panic

or anything else…weak. She must be strong, think what to do.

She needed to start doing something now, not simply stand by the side of the expressway and whine about her feet. She should go answer questions. The sooner the authorities got information, the sooner they could rescue her mother.

She took a step forward, and the marshal's phone rang. Wincing, she turned toward the car again and bent down to grab the cell phone from the console. Then, phone in hand, she trudged, wincing, toward the marshal and a policeman talking beside the road. The man who chased her was gone and more emergency vehicles had arrived, an ambulance among them. Traffic crawled, partly from a blocked lane, partly from the gapers.

"Halt right there, miss," the policeman called when Kristen was barely a dozen feet away from the Mustang.

Kristen held up the phone. "He got a phone call."

The deputy marshal spoke to the cop, who frowned, but nodded and started toward Kristen, the marshal beside him.

"This is the judge's daughter," the marshal spoke to the policeman.

"Kristen Lang," she supplied.

The cop's grass-green eyes, in a face pale enough to not have been exposed to the sun for the past year, raked over Kristen. "We need to talk to you."

"She's getting checked out by the paramedics first, then coming to the marshal's office," the deputy marshal said. "This is our jurisdiction."

"Then where are your men?" the cop demanded.

"On their way." The marshal looked at Kristen.

She ducked her head, feeling the revolting tangle of wet hair slap against her cheeks.

"Why don't you come to the ambulance?" the deputy marshal said. "I'll be right with you."

Apparently expecting her and the policeman to go along with this plan, he began to text on his phone.

Kristen hesitated. "I'd like to get my purse and phone out of my car."

"We need an accident report from her at the least," the policeman said.

"Since it was part of the kidnapping, we'll get it and pass it along."

Officer Green Eyes scowled but nodded and strode back toward one of the vehicles with flashing lights, each footfall looking hard enough to shake the earth.

"He doesn't know how to play with others." The deputy marshal smiled at Kristen.

She blinked. The grin transformed his face from hard authority, to boyish charm in a flash. An attractive flash.

"Now," he continued, "let's get you back out of the rain. You must be freezing." He hesitated, then held out his hand. "I'm Nick Sandoval, by the way."

She touched the tips of her fingers to his palm, finding it broad and firm, calloused as though he labored to earn his muscular frame rather than worked out in a gym. It was a hand one could hold onto and know one was safe.

She snapped her thoughts back to what was important. "I would like my phone, please." She sounded like a little girl asking for her favorite toy, not a grown woman with a master's degree in social work and a responsible job.

"I'll get it for you as soon as the crime scene techs release it. Her Honor may try to call it."

"With what? Her phone's still in the Camry." Tears stung Kristen's eyes. "I told her to put it down so it wouldn't knock her in the face when we crashed. It's my fault she doesn't have it."

"Her kidnappers would probably have taken it away from her anyway, Kristen." His tone was gentle, but his eyes were cold. She hadn't thought brown eyes could hold no warmth, but his looked like frozen Fudgsicles, nice on a hot day but uncomfortable in the chill of a summer storm.

"How will she call us if she doesn't have a phone?" Kristen asked.

"She'll find a way if anyone can." Nick touched her elbow. "Come on. You're not doing her any good standing here in the rain. The sooner we make sure you're all right and then get a statement from you, the sooner we can find her."

Kristen shook her head. "No paramedics. I'm just fine."

Except for her bruised and aching feet.

"You were in a crash bad enough for your air bags to deploy."

"The air bags going off is why I'm fine." She shifted from one foot to the other to ease pressure on her battered soles. "Please. I want to make my statement. I don't know much, but the sooner I tell you what I do know, the sooner you can find my mother."

Nick had no idea how the daughter of such a confident, powerful woman as Judge Julia Lang could walk as though she carried a hundred pound pack up a mountain, talk like the sound of her own voice frightened her and think she was to blame for that day's events. But she did look a body in the eye. Every time those lake-blue eyes of hers met his, he felt like someone Tasered him. Zing. Zing. Zap. The electric energy flowed from his neck to his toes.

In the office of the marshal service, Kristen Lang looked at him a great deal. Every time, she answered his questions precisely and concisely before she answered anyone else's, so much so that US Marshal Tom Callahan, his boss, sent him out of the room "So you'll stop being a distraction."

Nick didn't argue, but he figured he was a help, not a hindrance, and someone's ego was taking a hit at a time when egos over authority shouldn't matter. With a reassuring smile for Kristen, Nick left the room at a snail's pace and went into the hall.

Where he noticed the blood on the floor.

He shoved the door open. "Kristen, are you bleeding?"

She didn't meet his eyes this time. "Am I?" She glanced down, and her face whitened. "My feet. I knew they hurt, but—"

"Why didn't you tell the paramedics?" Callahan asked before Nick got the question out.

"This interview is far more important." If she was trying to smile, she failed. Her lips twisted, but more in a grimace of pain.

"Enough questions," Nick declared. "She needs to go to the hospital and have her feet seen to."

"My feet can wait. I need to answer all the questions I can to help find my mother." Her hands gripped the edge of the table, the short, polished nails digging into the fake wood, the knuckles white. "Even if it's my fault she was taken, it won't be my fault she isn't found."

"How many times do we have to tell you it's not your fault, Kristen?" Callahan sounded impatient. "From what you've said and what Her Honor texted, we know that you took every precautionary action you could under the circumstances."

"But I should never have been under the circumstances." This time, she focused those blue eyes on Callahan.

He didn't so much as blink at their impact.

"May I take her to get her feet seen to, sir?" Nick asked.

"Please do. And then drive her home and stay with her. Where is Her Honor's husband?"

"My father is in Switzerland," Kristen said.

"Business?" Nick asked, figuring on Zurich and Swiss bank accounts and all those things far above his touch or interest.

She shook her head. "Mountain climbing or something like that."

"Your father's on vacation without your mother?" Nick couldn't keep the astonishment from his tone.

He couldn't imagine his parents going on more than a weekend retreat without each other.

"Is that normal?"

"Abnormal would be if he did take a vacation with her." Her voice was flat as she looked at the table. "Has anyone called him?"

"We left a voice mail," Callahan said. "It's the middle of the night there, though."

Kristen nodded, then tried to stand. With a little cry, she fell back into her chair.

Callahan surged to his feet. "We'll call an ambulance. I'm so sorry we didn't realize sooner you were injured."

But they should have realized it. Nick should have. Someone, the paramedics if no one else, should have noticed she wore no shoes. His mother would have his hide for not being more careful with a lady who'd been in an accident and then run for her life down the side of the expressway.

"Please don't fuss over me.'" Her face was as white as the institutional walls around them. "I can walk."

"I don't think so." Nick glanced from his boss to Kristen. "With your permission, I'll carry you."

"You can't do that, Sandoval," Callahan protested.

"It's better than wasting resources others may need instead." Kristen offered the older man a tight smile, though her cheeks had flushed to the color of the strawberry Jell-O with whipped topping blended into it Nick's aunt Maggie insisted on bringing to every family gathering. "Just don't carry me over your shoulder. That's how that man…how he carried…me."

She pressed her hand to her mouth. For a moment, Nick feared she would be sick. Then he saw the tears welling in her eyes and realized she was holding back a sob.

If she were one of his sisters, he would pick her up and let her cry on his shoulder. She was, however, the daughter of a judge and the main witness to a serious crime perpetrated against that judge. He must maintain a professional demeanor which, sadly, included no comforting the victim.

Maybe he could take her home and let his mom do that.

Pretending he didn't see the tears, he picked her up from the chair, glad he worked out regularly. She was a big girl, not overweight, just tall and not model thin. She was just right in her proportions, as far as he was concerned.

"Is it all right if I put my arm around your neck?" she asked barely above a whisper.

He'd be flirting inappropriately if he gave the answer that sprang to mind—*A lady as pretty as you doesn't need permission to put her arm around me*—so he merely nodded and carried her outside to his car.

The rain had stopped. With rush hour passed, the streets were emptier, the office buildings and most of the restaurants except those around the theaters having closed for the night. Nothing was quiet, though. Buses still roared up the streets and the "L" trains rattled overhead. The sharp tang of wet pavement filled the air along with exhaust and cooking odors.

Nick was suddenly filled with a longing for the clean sweetness of rain-washed grass and dirt, his mother's roses fragrant from their bath, and even the earthy notes of wet dog. Wanting these scents in his nostrils meant he wanted to be home or visiting his parents, anywhere but facing the sort of trouble this night was still bound to bring, especially not an urgent care or hospital emergency room facility and the tedium of waiting in either.

He didn't realize he sighed until Kristen

removed her arm from around his neck and spoke. "I'm sure I can walk now."

"No way. It's just a few more feet to my car."

As in a half block to the parking garage, but he could manage, even if she was half again as heavy as his fiancée. His deceased fiancée. She'd been small-boned and fragile in too many ways, beyond his ability to save.

"I should have let your boss call an ambulance," Kristen said. "You don't need to go to all this trouble for me."

"I have orders to stay with you no matter what." Nick entered the parking garage and his Mustang was not far from the door.

The advantage of returning to work after most people had gone home.

"I have to set you down for a minute. Try to stand on your heels. I don't want oil or anything in those cuts." He released her from his hold.

"I think it's too late to worry about that now." Her tone was sharp. He didn't blame her. She was their only witness, their only hope at the moment of finding the judge, and they weren't taking care of her.

Despite her prickly response, she balanced on her heels, one hand resting on the black vinyl top of his convertible, her gaze focused on the street.

Nick unlocked the car and opened her door. "Here you go."

She didn't move except to fix her gaze on him. "Why did they take her?"

"If we figure that out, it will help us find her."

"Will there be a ransom?"

"That will help." Nick stepped away from the car, silently urging her to get in.

She did at last, and he closed the door. Once he was around the vehicle and seated beside her, she turned to him.

"I should have told someone about the SUV following me. That's why this is my fault. If I had mentioned that car when I got to the courthouse…"

"Provided the powers that be took you seriously."

"They would have taken my mom seriously."

"If she had told us she had a concern, which she did not." He started the Mustang and headed for the exit. "We don't even know for sure she had concerns, just your suspicions of it."

"I know. And it makes no sense she wouldn't say something to the marshal service. She's very security conscious. Still…" She speared her fingers into her hair and sighed. "Then again, she wouldn't want to look silly if it came to nothing." She rested her hands on her cheeks. "It's all pointless now."

"Except for future reference."

"If she has a future." Her voice did that strangled squeaky thing that told Nick she was worried or frightened or probably both.

"We'll see to it she has a future, Kristen."

She gazed out the window. "Where are you taking me?"

"To the hospital on Harrison. The urgent care centers all seem to be closed by now."

Nine o'clock. The judge had been gone for three hours. She might be dead. Surely they were foolish criminals if they believed they would get away with harming a hair on a federal judge. But if law enforcement heard nothing within the next few hours, Nick feared for Her Honor.

If he could have taken after that SUV instead of babysitting one perpetrator and the daughter, he might have caught them. Probably not in the traffic, but possibly.

First he would get Kristen's feet seen to and then take her home, wherever she lived. Federal agents would already be setting up at the judge's house awaiting a ransom call or some kind of demand from the kidnapper. Once Kristen was there, Nick was free to go home.

Home sounded wonderful. Food. His cat. A comfortable chair in which to relax.

As if he could with the judge missing and this lovely young woman castigating herself over that disappearance.

Maybe he should take her to his parents' house, if Callahan would allow it. Miss Kristen Lang shouldn't be alone. He would ask. First, he would get her to the emergency room.

With light traffic, they reached the hospital two miles away in no time. On a weeknight the emergency room wasn't busy. Shortly after their arrival, Kristen was in a wheelchair and whisked to a bed.

"You can go now," she told him. "I can call someone to take me home."

"Sorry, but I can't leave you until you're home." Nick crossed his arms and leaned against the wall.

"Is she a prisoner?" a nurse asked.

"She's a victim under protective custody for the moment. But just her feet need taken care of."

The nurse asked Kristen if that was true. When she nodded, shooting Nick a glare, a doctor came in, looked at her battered feet, then issued orders. The staff got to work cleansing, bandaging, giving tetanus and antibiotic shots. Through it all, Kristen lay on the gurney with her face a mask, her eyes squeezed shut, and Nick remained in his stance against the wall—

Until his cell rang.

"Excuse me." He started to leave the cubicle.

Kristen shot upright and grabbed his arm. "Is it to do with my mother?"

"I won't know until I answer." Nick patted her hand and slipped down the corridor.

The call *was* about her mother. What Nick learned left him leaning against another wall, his hands balled into fists at his sides, every calming technique he knew employed to make him appear passive when he returned to Kristen.

Those blue eyes collided with his the instant he stepped into her cubicle. "What?" Her voice was a mere breath.

"Not until we're away from here."

He wasn't discussing this in front of hospital personnel or patients.

"We're done." Kristen swung her legs over the side of the gurney.

The nurse appeared from nowhere. "You can't walk on those feet."

"I can't stay. I must get out of here. I can't… I won't…" She pressed her hand to her chest, her words growing faster, her breathing shallow.

"I'll get the doctor." The nurse sped off on nearly silent feet.

"Easy there." Nick clasped Kristen's hands in his. "If you have a panic attack, they may admit you."

"I can't breathe in here." She tugged one hand free and clutched at her throat.

"I'll fetch a chair." Nick released her other hand and found a wheelchair in the corridor.

"You can't take that," an orderly called down the hallway.

Nick ignored him and helped Kristen into the chair. With the orderly and nurse calling after them, Nick whisked Kristen from the emergency room and out to his car. His credentials had stopped security from having his vehicle towed, so they didn't have far to go. In moments, Kristen was buckled into the passenger seat and Nick behind the wheel.

He only drove as far as the exit before pulling over and turning to Kristen. "We've heard a ransom demand of sorts."

"Of sorts? What does that mean?" Her blue eyes were enormous dark pools in the glow of the dashboard and security lights. "Too little money to be legitimate? Passage out of the country?"

"You."

"I beg your pardon?"

Nick took a deep breath, nearly choking on the lingering odors of the hospital clinging to them—and the words he had to impart to this lovely, anxious woman. "The kidnappers called your phone while it was in the marshal's office. They want you in exchange for your mother alive."

THREE

Kristen didn't have time to fall apart. As much as she wanted to crumple into as small a ball as a woman who was five feet ten inches could, she understood with the sensible part of her brain she must remain calm, composed, logical.

The rest of her brain shoved the sensible bit aside like a snowplow clearing a road and barreled over any notions of not drawing in on herself. She pulled her knees to her chest, a tight fit in the sports car. With her shins resting against the glove compartment she could barely wrap her arms around her knees and lower her head. Her hair, a tangled, still-damp mass, curtained her face so she didn't have to look at headlights flashing by on the street or Nick's face displaying what was more than likely impatience or disgust.

The sensible portion of Kristen's brain registered impatience and disgust with her upright fetal position. But they were weakly expressed emotions, too feeble to overpower the deep aching horror ripping a hole in her heart and through to her soul.

Two men had kidnapped her mother instead of her. Yet they wanted her, not her mother.

"I should have known something was up when that SUV kept following me." The words squeezed out of her constricted throat. "I should have told you about it. I should have told Mom about it. But I couldn't think why anyone would want me. I still don't know why. Now…if anything happens to her…" She couldn't continue with the thought. She couldn't think about anything happening to her mother, especially when that anything would be her fault.

"Kristen." Nick's voice was low and gentle, calming. "We are doing everything we can to ensure nothing happens to your mother."

"They want me." She spoke to her lap. "You can get my mother back by giving them me."

"Out of the question."

Of course it was. No one would think of giving criminals what they wanted—her. Her, a nobody, with her unimportant—by the world's standards—job. Two men wanted her so badly they risked kidnapping a federal judge in an attempt to get Kristen in the bargain, though she couldn't imagine why. She must be forgetting something, but in trying to recall anything she had said or done that would anger criminals to such an extent, her head spun like a lazy Susan full of sand rather than spices.

The smallness of the car struck her then, how the seat pressed against her back, the dashboard against her legs and the door against her side. The car was too small for two taller-than-average adults, especially when one of them was a broad-shouldered male. He took up too much of the space, too much of the oxygen. She could not breathe.

"Air." She gasped like someone who had been under water too long. "I need air."

Her hand dropped to the door handle. She flipped it open and scrambled from the car. Her sore feet inside the slipper socks the hospital provided hit the pavement too hard. The air smelled of exhaust from the nearby road, and wet concrete. But a stiff breeze blew the clouds from the sky and flowed around her like a warm, gentle touch, and her lungs expanded. She straightened, inhaled, and ran away from the confines of the car to—what?

Something. She needed to get to something. Her condo so she could be alone and think and figure out why anyone wanted to kidnap her. To her office where she could look at her case files and figure out who might want to harm her. Back to the US marshal's office to find out how she could trade herself for her mother's freedom. She ran across the nearly empty parking lot and the lure of the nearby "L" station for a train she couldn't ride because she didn't have her purse for her transit pass nor her phone to access electronic tickets on the commuter train.

She didn't even have her office or condo keys. She didn't have her handbag back yet.

She realized at that moment she was crying. She stumbled to a halt beside a light pole. It was something to lean against, but it was cold and indifferent to how her insides felt, shredded.

Footfalls sounded behind her. She supposed she should have flinched or taken off running again. After all, criminals wanted her and she had just stupidly run across a deserted parking lot at night. But she didn't move. She knew who was racing after her, the deputy marshal whose broad shoulder would be so much nicer to lean on than the light pole, if he weren't a man in uniform, or a suit, or any other symbol of a man one couldn't count on to be around when needed.

He was there at that moment, though.

"I'm all right," she said to ward him off. "I just needed air."

"I understand. My car's a little small. But

I don't think this is the best place to get your supply of oxygen."

So soothing. So reasonable.

She wanted to shout, *I let my mother get kidnapped instead of me. Don't be so nice to me.*

"Let's get you someplace comfortable."

"I want to go home."

He hesitated a moment before saying what she knew he would. "I'm afraid I can't let you go home right now."

"Is it a crime scene?"

"Not at all, but it could be watched to see if you show up."

Of course it could.

She wrapped her arms around herself, annoyed she hadn't thought of that, shivering from the prospect that someone could remove her from her home without guaranteeing that her mother would go free.

"Then where will I go?" she asked. "You won't lock me up somewhere will you?"

"We do have houses—"

"No." She faced him, hands up as though she could push him away. "I can't be locked up somewhere. I have to do something. I have to get my mom back."

"We will, but we need your help to know why someone wants to abduct you."

"I don't know. I honestly don't know. In

spite of that SUV following me from work, I thought it was my mother who was the target. She seemed odd in the car. I thought she knew something. I thought—I've told you what I thought."

Nick nodded. His head was bowed over his phone, and he was texting, thumbs flying over the screen. The tone of incoming texts rang in continuous staccato bursts.

Kristen glared at him more because she wanted her phone, her line to communicating with her friends, than because he wasn't giving her any attention. She didn't need his attention, especially if what he was doing meant her mother's safe return. She hoped those texts had nothing to do with locking her away somewhere for her own good. What was good for her might not be good for her mother.

Her feet hurting, she leaned against the pole and raised one leg to tuck her foot behind her knee and rest it. After a few moments, she switched legs.

Nick glanced at her. "I'm sorry. I'm making arrangements and getting updates."

"Which are?"

"I'm taking you to my sister's house."

"I mean the updates."

His sister's house sounded as bad as a lockup.

The marshal and his family were strangers she didn't know if she could trust.

"We can pick up your phone and purse." Nick slid his phone into his pocket.

Kristen stared at him. "That's your update? You all have nothing else?"

"We thought we had the license plate of the SUV that took your mom."

Kristen straightened. "That's good news, isn't it? Can't you trace it?"

"We did. The plate doesn't match the description of the vehicle."

"Stolen?"

"The license plate was. We don't know about the vehicle." He held out his hand as though he expected her to take it and let him lead her back to his car as he started to walk forward. "Let's go get your phone, then get you someplace safe and comfortable."

"Why is your sister's house safe?"

"Her husband's a former cop who's now a home security systems salesman."

"I can't impose on strangers." She fell into step beside him, only wincing slightly.

"No one is a stranger to my sister."

"She's a stranger to me."

"So am I, but you got in my car willingly several times now." He flashed her a grin.

Her toes curled inside the rubber-soled socks. "That's different. You're law enforcement."

"Fair enough." They reached the car and he held the still open passenger door. "I can leave you at the marshal's office when we stop for your phone and purse. They will take you to a safe house to wait until we free Her Honor."

She would be locked into a safe house for her own good. She knew that. She was a victims' advocate and had reluctantly sent clients to such places for their protection, witnesses to horrendous crimes. People the Marshals Service had helped her make disappear. Now the marshals wanted to help her disappear for a while. A short while, she hoped.

She glared at Nick—up at Nick. At five feet ten inches, she didn't get to look up with many men.

She dropped her gaze to remember the uniform and why she was with him in the first place. "I think I'm being manipulated, except I don't know why you would prefer I go to your sister. If bad guys are after me, isn't she in danger, security husband or not?"

"It's such a small risk anyone will trace you there, she's willing to take it." He released the door. "But let's get going. This parking lot is too exposed, and we've been here too long."

She took the message for what it was—*we*

might be watched—and slid into the Mustang. Nick closed her door before she reached for the handle, then rounded the hood to the driver's side.

They said nothing on the two-mile drive back to the marshal's office, a quick trip at night with relatively little traffic on the road. Despite him running the air-conditioning, Kristen kept her window down for the free flow of air. She could think better with uncirculated air in her face. Yet thinking meant feeling and feeling brought guilt.

She had done something that made bad guys want to harm her. They didn't want a ransom. If so, they wouldn't want her as exchange for her mother. Mom was worth more on the ransom market than Kristen.

She didn't know what the men wanted. She only knew their actions fell on her shoulders, were her fault, and she needed to find a way to stop them. She would find it regardless of the consequences.

Nick didn't like Kristen's silence. He liked her panic even less. She was strong-looking in appearance, gorgeous with those lake-blue eyes, high cheekbones and athletic build. Yet Kristen's appearance was deceiving. She was as fragile in her spirit as petite Michele, his deceased fiancée, had been, maybe more so. Michele had come across as confident in her worth, in her belief others' kindnesses to her were deserved. And they had been. Michele was one of the most giving people he knew, a true servant of the Lord's.

Yet in the end, that open heart of hers had been her undoing. She thought she was safe no matter what part of the city she ventured into because she helped so many people in need. Michele had trusted God to keep her safe. She had trusted the wrong people, and they had killed her. Nick suspected Kristen trusted no one, which might be just as dangerous to her safety as believing in the goodness of others.

Or that God would take care of her.

Nick shook off that thought. His family had been helping him to regain his faith since Michele's death. Yet sometimes, doubt reared its ugly head.

Kristen was not Michele. Kristen was strictly business. He was assigned to protect her. Protect her he would—with his life if necessary. He would not fail her as he had failed to be with Michele when she needed him most.

He had failed her. God hadn't.

Along the lines of protecting Kristen, Nick pulled into the parking garage, but texted for someone to bring her personal items to them.

She didn't need to be walking on her battered feet. That meant the two of them sat in his car, Nick vigilant for all the garage was secure, and Kristen silent, still gazing out the window until another deputy marshal brought her purse and two laptop computers, her mother's and hers, to the car. She thanked the courier, then fell silent again until Nick pulled onto the street.

"They're not going to question me further now that they know these men are after me and not my mother?" Kristen spoke at last.

"They will, but not until tomorrow." He headed to Lake Shore Drive and the north end of the city.

Beside him, Kristen clutched her hands on her knees. "Isn't that too late? Wouldn't talking to me tonight help them find her sooner?"

"Do you know any reason why someone would want to harm you?" He countered her question with a question, the obvious question she had surely been asking herself since he informed her of what they had heard from the kidnappers.

She shook her head. "I can look on my computer, search case files for possibilities."

"But you can't share that information with us because of confidentiality laws, right?"

"Right."

"So we need to see what the kidnappers' demands are."

"But you know already. They want me." She bent her head and muttered something like, "And they can have me."

Nick inhaled the clean, crisp scent of the lake blowing through the open passenger window. "Of course they can't have you. We would never exchange one person for another. And right now, we don't even know where they want to make such an exchange."

"And when we do?"

"When the Marshals Service knows, they will act appropriately." He wanted to offer her some comfort, something proactive. "Meanwhile, think of someone who holds a grudge against you so we can get permission for you to release that information."

She needed to eat and rest, if he could get her to do either. He hoped his sister Gina, could. She was good at persuading people to do what was best for them. She had brought him back from the brink after his fiancée's death.

Call it what it is—her murder.

Killed because he had been working and couldn't help her when she got a flat tire, and she walked to an "L" station.

He understood how Kristen must be feeling at that moment. He supposed that was why his boss had assigned Nick to watch over her, to protect her. Callahan knew Nick would give her sympathy, even empathy.

He wondered if he should tell her about Michele. Twice before their exit, he opened his mouth to say he knew how she felt, but closed it again. Gina might have forced him to eat and rejoin the world, to keep going until the grief eased, but she hadn't been able to get him to talk about Michele to anyone. Those thoughts and feelings were between him and God. He wasn't going to change anything with a lady he barely knew and was unlikely to see again in twenty-four hours, except on a wholly passing way if she came to the courthouse.

"The waiting is terrible," he said at last.

She nodded.

"And you keep thinking about what you could have done differently."

"I could have stayed with her instead of running."

Nick flipped on his blinker to take them into the heart of the Lakeview neighborhood. "What good would that have done?"

"They would have let her go if they had me." She pressed her hands to her cheeks. "I would know they weren't hurting her."

"Or they would have kept you both and harmed you both."

Nick wished he knew her well enough to know how she would react if he touched her hand, her shoulder, gave her that bit of human contact so comforting in times of distress. He didn't know her, though, so kept his distance.

Off a more major thoroughfare, he turned onto a relatively quiet street and stopped in front of a four-flat building with a carriage house behind. "My sister and her husband live in the carriage house."

"I wanted to live in a carriage house, but I could never find one I could afford." She popped open her door and climbed out before he could reach her side. "Can you park here?"

"They'll have a sticker for me." Nick gathered up her belongings, such as they were, and carried them through the open gate. "I'm going to ask Sean, my brother-in-law, to lock this for the night."

Kristen stared at him. In the light of the security lamps, her face was sickly pale. "You don't think I'm safe here."

"Kristen—" He stopped.

Her wide-eyed horror roused his sympathy so much, he doubted he could keep an emotional distance from her.

"Kristen," he began again, "I don't think you're safe anywhere. This is just the best place at the moment if you don't want to be locked away in a safe house until we hear more from the kidnappers."

As if to respond to his statement, a cell phone rang. Kristen jumped. Nick reached for his phone. Nothing showed on the screen, and the ringing continued.

"It's mine." She was fumbling in her bag. A pack of tissues, a tube of lip balm and three peppermints landed on the sidewalk before she drew the phone from the suitcase she called a purse.

"Let me." Nick held out his hand.

But she was already answering. "Hello?"

She lowered the phone so it switched to speaker mode, and Nick heard the response as clearly as she did.

"Please," said a whispery voice, "do whatever they say. They'll kill me otherwise."

"Mom? Is that you? What are they—?"

A scream interrupted her, and then the call was disconnected.

FOUR

The phone slipped from Kristen's nerveless fingers. Nick caught it before it hit the pavement. He stared at the screen. She stared at him. His face was grim. Hers felt bloodless, nerveless, stiff. She thought she might be sick or cry again or, worst of all, fling herself against Nick's broad chest and cling to him as the only thing in her world that appeared solid.

"Blocked call." Nick sounded matter-of-fact.

Of course he did. This was his job. He dealt in potential danger or the real thing every day.

"Let's get you inside." He held his hand out to her as he had in the parking lot, a kind gesture of support.

She took it, holding on perhaps a little too tightly. "My mom—" That was all she managed through her constricted throat.

She sounded like a lost child and wanted to kick herself for not being stronger in this crisis.

"We don't know that was your mother." Nick paused and looked behind them.

Checking for someone lurking in the shadows between streetlights?

All was quiet save for a bass guitar thumping from inside the building to their right and the distant rumble of the elevated train a couple blocks away. Nothing moved but tree branches in a light breeze, but those movements created shadows, and Kristen wanted to race into the carriage house tucked behind the block of four apartments.

A light burned over the front door of the house and more light shone behind filmy curtains at the windows. Light spoke of welcome, shelter, rest. Kristen would love all those things if not for that scream echoing through her skull.

"I can't imagine my mother screaming, but someone can be made to scream against their will." She admitted the truth.

"They can under duress." Still holding her hand, his fingers warm and strong, Nick led the way up the steps of the porch.

The minute their footfalls echoed on the boards, the front door opened to a rush of cooled air and a spill of lamplight. "Nick, you made it at last."

The woman standing in the doorway was probably a decade older than Kristen's twenty-five, and as pretty as her brother was handsome, with her long, dark hair in a ponytail, her deep brown eyes and sculptured cheekbones. She smiled with a warmth that put the summer night to shame. "Hi, I'm Gina. Come on in and let me feed you."

"You don't need to go to any trouble on my behalf." Kristen doubted she could eat.

"No trouble." She fixed her eyes on Nick. "Speaking of trouble, our big sister says you're in trouble for not calling her to say you're not coming to dinner after all."

"I forgot." Nick's ears looked red. "Now may we come in before you assassinate my character in front of Kristen?"

Not an assassination to Kristen, just a confirmation. She knew all about jobs that made men unreliable for showing up to dinner. Her father had been that way all her life. Once she tried to get him home early. She was learning to cook and made him a special meal for his birthday. He promised to be home. He arrived long after she had placed everything in the refrigerator, washed the dishes and gone to bed. An emergency at work had been her father's excuse, his apology accompanied by a gift certificate to her favorite store. Not even a gift.

Kristen felt an odd urge to ask Gina if her

husband came home to dinner when he said he would, unlike her brother.

"Are you going to introduce me to your guest?" Gina asked.

"This is Kristen Lang." Nick stepped back so Kristen could precede him into the house.

The door opened directly into a living room with lovely hardwood floors and big windows sheltered from view of buildings too close by draping greenery inside and out. An archway led into a small dining room and kitchen beyond, where a man was rounding the corner from a hallway, leaning on a cane, though he was probably the same age as Gina.

Nick's brother-in-law, the former cop. Kristen guessed all she needed to know. Wounded on the job. Left for security analysis work.

She offered him a smile.

"I'm old-fashioned enough to ask if we can call you Kristen?" he asked, returning her smile.

Despite lines of pain on his face, he appeared as welcoming as his wife.

Tears pricked Kristen's eyes for the show of kindness from these strangers. She swallowed twice before she could speak. "Please do."

"I should have asked if it's all right." Nick rubbed his chin with his knuckles. "I just associate Lang with your mother."

The knowledge shouldn't have bothered her, but it did. Once more, her powerful mother overshadowed her.

Her powerful mother who may have been forced to scream. Her powerful father who hadn't answered his phone when she'd called.

She should call him again. She now knew his number by heart, she had made sure of it once she had her phone in her hands again. She wanted to be able to call her father even if Nick or anyone else held her phone again.

"Let me show you to a room and then you can have something to eat, and rest." Gina touched Kristen's arm. "Do you have anything to wear other than that dress?"

Kristen shook her head. "I haven't been home. I live in the western suburbs."

"And there are now marshals there," Nick added. "And at her mother's house."

Kristen startled, though she knew she should have figured this out. Law enforcement would be waiting to see if anyone tried to reach them.

"You're taller than I am, but I can find you something that'll work."

In no time, Gina found sweatpants and a T-shirt and left Kristen to wash and change.

Self-conscious among these strangers, Kristen made herself more presentable, then moved to the end of the hallway and stood at the opening to the kitchen. Gina was setting the table. Her husband was already seated there with an iPad propped beside a mug in front of him. Nick was nowhere to be seen.

"Come in, Kristen," Gina said without looking up. "I have lasagna heating and here's a salad."

Kristen wanted to say she wasn't hungry. Her stomach was knotted like a pretzel. But she needed to eat. If she had to run, she should have fuel.

She moved toward the table. "Where's Nick?"

"Securing the perimeter." Sean glanced from his iPad. "It'll make our tenants angry to have to use their key cards on the gate, but we need to keep you safe."

"We have cameras all around the property," Gina added. "This is mostly a safe neighborhood, but one never knows nowadays." She pulled a roasting dish from the oven.

Despite her knotted stomach, Kristen's mouth watered at the aroma of garlic and melted cheese.

"Tell Nick to get in here," Gina told her husband.

Sean tapped the screen of his tablet. "He's on the porch talking on the phone."

"Phone?" Kristen pushed away from the table and hobbled to the door as fast as her feet allowed. She started to yank open the door, then wondered if Nick would stop talking if she did, so she leaned against the panel instead and tried to hear the conversation on the other side.

"Yes, of course I have her phone." He sounded impatient. "No, I won't let her—"

A passing motorcycle drowned his words.

"Let me know if anything comes in on the judge's phone, of course." The next remark was clear. "I'll tell her tomorrow."

Kristen yanked open the door. "You'll tell me what tomorrow?"

Nick grimaced and slipped the phone into his pocket. "I'm hoping it'll be a moot point tomorrow. Now let's eat."

"You don't trust me?" Kristen persisted.

Nick said nothing.

"I'm useless to you if you don't trust me."

"It's my job to be cautious." Nick's voice was soft, almost tender, his words as good as an answer confirming her suspicions.

Kristen bowed her head. "I'm a disappointment to my parents."

The confession slipped out, something she would never have admitted to a stranger under normal circumstances.

"I doubt—"

"Stop." Kristen held up a staying hand. "I

don't want platitudes about how you're sure that's not true."

"Are you two coming before this food gets cold and the cheese dries to dust?" Gina called from the dining room.

Kristen slipped past Nick and headed for a meal she believed she didn't want. But when she sat before the plate of lasagna, a crisp salad and crusty bread, she discovered she was hungry. While conversation flowed between Nick, his sister and brother-in-law, light banter over baseball scores and an anecdote about one of their nephews, Kristen kept silent, listened and ate. Then, halfway through the meal, she wondered if her mother was getting fed anything, and Kristen's appetite fled. With care, she set her fork on the side of her plate and dropped her hands to her lap.

"Have enough?" Gina asked.

Kristen nodded.

"Then feel free to go to your room," Gina said.

Everyone wished Kristen good-night. She stumbled down the hallway, readied herself for bed and slid between the sheets. She took the time to pray for Mom's safety, then began to wonder how she would learn what the kidnappers wanted. How would she get her phone back from Nick? They had called her on it twice now. They might call her on it again. They wanted her.

Why? Why? Why?

She needed her client records. All of them, not just the ones she had been working on so they were on her computer. Along mundane lines, she needed clothes to wear that fit. She needed to be on her own and not watched every minute.

She needed sleep, but it eluded her beyond short intervals. She drifted off, then a memory, a dream, perhaps a sound from outside, jerked her awake to lie listening to the hiss of the cooled air through the vent overhead and a distant siren.

At last, with the waking of birds and increase of street noise, she gave up trying to sleep. She made herself as presentable as she could and slipped down the hall to the kitchen. Sean sat at the dining table, again with an iPad and cup of coffee in front of him. He smiled at her and indicated the coffee carafe beside him and mugs on the kitchen counter. Kristen grabbed a mug and started for the carafe. Sean swiped the screen of the tablet, but not before Kristen read the blazing headlines on the news app.

"Federal Judge Kidnapped"

"Daughter's Involvement Suspected"

* * *

Nick saw Kristen sway as he entered the kitchen. In a bound, he grasped her shoulders. "Are you okay?"

"Okay? Of course I'm not okay." She jabbed her finger toward Sean's iPad and the glaring headline. "What's that mean? How can I be a suspect in my own mother's kidnapping?"

"I don't know. No one bothered to tell me… anything…" He trailed off as his phone rang.

He pulled it from his pocket. Callahan. His boss didn't wait for Nick to say hello before he began talking.

"If you haven't seen the morning news, don't turn it on. I don't want her to see—"

"Too late, sir." Realizing he still rested one hand on Kristen's shoulder, Nick backed away. "What's going on?"

"We don't know. We had nothing to do with this." Callahan sounded tired and frustrated, rather like Nick felt. "But whoever planted this with journalists is no petty criminal. We're dealing with people with power."

"Why would they want people to think I'm a suspect?" Kristen demanded, apparently able to hear Callahan through the phone.

"We don't know," Callahan answered. "But I think it's all the more reason why she needs to be someplace safer than your sister's house.

These people have a plan they're not letting us in on."

"And you're not going to leave me out of it when they do," Kristen said, drowning out Callahan's next words.

Nick held up his free hand and slipped into Sean's home office, where he could close the door. "We can't force her to go, sir."

"We can go along with the suspect angle and lock her up."

"You can only hold her for twenty-four hours unless you can arrest her, and there's no cause for her to be under arrest."

Callahan growled.

"Let's stick with the current plan, sir. I have her phone. If anyone calls, I'll give it to her to answer and monitor the call."

"I'm counting on you not to fail, Sandoval." Callahan was back to sounding weary.

Nick said goodbye and returned to the dining room to find Kristen seated at the table, her chin resting in her hands and a cup of untouched coffee before her. Her eyes, such a beautiful blue, appeared a little glassy, as though she stared into the distance beyond the greenery and brick wall outside the windows. Sean and his tablet were gone, but singing inside the master bathroom suggested Gina was awake and ready to join them.

"May I have some of this coffee?" Nick picked up the carafe to see if it held anything.

Kristen shrugged, then removed her elbows from the table and sat up. "My mother would be appalled to see me with my elbows on the table."

"You're not eating, so we'll let it slip." Nick offered her a smile.

She didn't respond.

"But you're about to eat," Nick continued. "Gina's awake, and her life is centered around feeding people."

"I'm not hungry."

"I mean literally. She's a professional chef."

Kristen's eyes flicked to the rather small kitchen, and one eyebrow arched.

"They like living in the city close to work, so this is the sacrifice she makes."

"A gnat-sized kitchen." Gina blew into the kitchen on a cloud of steam, her hair curling from the band holding it in a ponytail. "But I still make the best omelet you'll ever eat. What do you want in it? And don't tell me you're not hungry."

"I am," Nick said.

"May I have my phone?" Kristen held out her hand. "I need to try my father again."

Nick pulled her phone from his pocket, ready

for the fight. "What's his number. I'll put it in for you."

"I can't make my own phone calls?" Kristen narrowed her eyes, intensifying their blue.

"I'm afraid not."

"Because I'm a suspect?"

"Not to our knowledge, and we should know if you were since you're in our custody."

She flinched visibly at that word.

"Protection," Nick corrected himself. "Someone fed that information to the media, and we don't know who or why."

"To make me less sympathetic." She rose and began to pace between the front door and the dining room archway. "I've seen this with victims before. The other party tries to assassinate their character to make whatever happened to them appear less horrendous."

"I've never even asked. Are you a lawyer too?"

"On the contrary. I'm a social worker, a victims' advocate to be precise. I know what happens to those harmed by crimes and how too many others treat them. You know—the spouse who's abused is accused of neglecting her husband or being a terrible mother. The college girl who's assaulted has loose morals. My mother is kidnapped and saves me from the same fate, and I'm accused of being involved so I am a terrible person who doesn't deserve to have anyone care about what happens to me if these men get to me."

Nick gazed at her in awe. Despite her borrowed and ill-fitting clothes, her hair pulled up in a messy ponytail, she looked rather magnificent striding about his sister's house. The longer she talked, the straighter her shoulders grew, emphasizing her graceful height. Her strides lengthened. Her eyes shone like Lake Michigan in full sunlight.

He had thought her pretty the day before. At that moment, to him, she was possibly the most beautiful woman he had ever seen.

Which scared him more than any criminal ever had.

If Gina hadn't entered the room at that moment carrying plates filled with omelets and fresh fruit, Nick might have run for the nearest hills, something not easy to find in the flat Midwest.

"Orange juice and fresh coffee coming up." Gina set the plates on the table. "Eat. They're avocado, bacon and cheese."

"They look amazing." Kristen slid onto her chair and picked up a fork.

"You'd better eat," Nick told her. "Gina might force-feed you otherwise."

"I'd better eat if I—" She stopped talking and speared a strawberry.

Nick waited for her to finish her sentence, while he dug into his own breakfast. She never did continue, but ate with mechanical precision like someone fueling a machine rather than enjoying every tasty bite.

Fueling a machine. A machine that might have to run at any moment.

"Don't do it, Kristen," Nick said.

"Don't do what?" Her face was too innocent, too bland.

Nick frowned. "Don't even think about running away."

"I can't. You won't let me take my phone and then I won't know where they took my mom."

Too quick, too pat an answer.

She was up to something. Or she was thinking about doing something. He rubbed the back of his neck as though he truly possessed hairs there that could stand like a dog's hackles. He needed to watch her every move. As much as possible, he wouldn't allow her to be alone, and he wouldn't let her phone out of his sight.

As though she sensed his distrust, Kristen rose, her plate in hand. "I'll take your dishes too. Gina shouldn't have to clean up as well as cook."

"I never clean up," Gina called from the kitchen.

Nick rose and entered the room with Kristen. His sister stood at the counter chopping fresh herbs. "The fallback of all working women—a slow cooker." Gina flashed them a smile. "This should be ready by six o'clock. I'll be home by ten."

"Just tell me what else needs to be done," Kristen said. "I'm not restaurant kitchen caliber, but I'm a pretty good cook anyway."

The women began rattling off ingredients and instructions. Nick slid onto a stool at the breakfast bar and listened and watched. He wasn't a bad chef himself, thanks to his mom and sister, but Kristen seemed to relax under Gina's warmth and care, unlike how she was with him—distant and tense.

Gina left Kristen caramelizing onions and slipped into Sean's office.

Nick rose. "What can I do to help?"

"Tuck those herbs under the skin of the chicken?" Kristen flicked a glance to the sliced chicken on a cutting board and then to where he had left their cells side by side on the bar.

He expected her to ask him something about her situation, but she turned back to the fragrant onions. "Don't they have children?" Her voice was barely audible. "Or is it none of my business?"

"We're a pretty open family, so I can tell

you. Gina can't have kids, so they're waiting to adopt now that Sean's business is doing well."

"That's wonderful. I mean about adopting." She stirred the onions with too much vigor, sending a few pieces to sizzle on the stove top. "So you have two older sisters?"

"And brothers." Nick wrinkled his nose and began to tuck the chopped herbs beneath the chicken skin, trying not to feel the rubbery texture of the raw meat. "I'm the baby."

"Better than being the only."

"Uh-huh. Do you want to trade jobs?"

She glanced at him. "What's wrong?"

"I hate the feel of raw meat."

"Seriously?" She laughed, a genuine ripple of humor straight from her lungs. "You didn't flinch when you saw my bloody feet, but raw chicken makes you squeamish?"

"Yep. I fully admit it."

And the weakness was worth it to hear that laugh. The sound warmed the overly air-conditioned room.

"Okay, we'll trade."

Nick washed his hands probably longer than necessary, then took over the sautéing. "How are your feet?"

"They're improved, but I wish I had a good pair of flip-flops, something thick and soft." She looked at her phone. "Any chance we can go to my house so I can get some clothes of my own?"

"Maybe someone can bring you some." Nick turned off the flame and scraped the onions into a waiting bowl.

"The idea of a stranger going through my things doesn't make me happy, but if it's the only way…" She fell silent for a moment, glaring at him. "They already have, haven't they?"

"There could have been clues." He defended the agency's actions.

"And you wonder why the media called me a suspect when you're treating me like one?" She began to throw the chicken pieces into the slow cooker with more vigor than necessary.

"I'm sorry." He didn't know what else to say. She knew the action was necessary.

"I'll get someone to bring you clothes. Do you want to make a list? I can email it."

"Thank you. Let me finish putting this food together." She elbowed him aside in the tiny galley kitchen, then proceeded to stir ingredients into the pot with an economy of movement that said she had performed such actions many times.

Nick retreated to his stool and texted Callahan about getting a female marshal to pick up clothes and whatever else Kristen wanted.

Within a quarter hour, Kristen had made a list and Nick passed it along.

Then the day stretched before them with Sean working in his office, Gina heading off to the nearby restaurant where she worked and Kristen's cell phone lying on the coffee table in the center of the living room where she and Nick retreated.

Her phone wasn't silent. In truth, it rang or pinged with incoming texts so often she set it to silent. Her office wanted to know if she was coming into work. What appeared to be friends texted to see if she was all right and what was going on. To each, under Nick's instruction, she responded that she couldn't talk about the situation, but she was safe and well.

After texting this for perhaps the tenth time, she glanced at Nick, a crease between her smooth, dark gold eyebrows. "What if these men have access to the tower to triangulate where my phone is located?"

"It's not likely they'd find exactly where you are. Lakeview is pretty densely populated. But Sean has this house under constant surveillance from outdoor cameras." Nick hesitated then told her what he had learned from his own messages. "But because that is not an impossibility, you will have to go somewhere else tomorrow morning if we haven't heard from the kidnappers."

"And if we have?" Her gaze challenged him.

He shrugged. "You'll still have to go somewhere else."

She nodded and picked up a paperback novel from a stack on a side table. Nick read the news on his phone and tried not to fall asleep. At lunchtime, Sean emerged from his office to offer to make sandwiches. Kristen leaped up and took over the duty. Before they finished eating, a series of beeps rang from the office and Sean went to check on the alarm.

"We're about to have company," he announced upon his return to the dining room.

A moment later, one of the female marshals knocked on the door. She wheeled a suitcase. "Where's your computer?" she asked without giving anyone a greeting.

"What do you need my computer for?" Kristen asked.

"It shouldn't have been given back to you. We need to take it to our office, Kristen." The deputy marshal, who Nick didn't know, looked at Nick rather than Kristen. "We need to look for clues."

"That information is private." Kristen gripped the retractable handle of her suitcase so hard Nick was sure she would rip it out of its track. "I work on client files on that computer."

"That's what we need to look at," the deputy marshal said.

Kristen was shaking her head before the woman finished her brief explanation. "No one looks at those files other than me without the permission of each of our clients or a warrant."

"Then we'll get a warrant." The deputy marshal left with a none-too-gentle closing of the door.

Without a word, Kristen stalked into the guest room and shut the door behind her. Despite outside cameras, Nick watched the door as though she could slip away.

In a few minutes, she emerged wearing jeans and a T-shirt that fit her, along with thong sandals that probably felt better on her sore feet than flat slippers. Still not speaking, she went straight to her phone and checked for messages.

When she glanced up, her eyes were wet.

"What's wrong?" Nick held out his hand, wanting the phone.

Instead, she gripped his fingers. "It's from my father's secretary. She can't reach him either."

Nick let her hold his hand. "Is that unusual?"

"My father had a cell phone all my life. It's never far from his hand."

"Where is he?" Nick tried to sound calm, as if interested only out of politeness, while his mind spun over the possibility that the kid-napping of Judge Lang and saying they really wanted Kristen was a ruse. Her father wouldn't be the first spouse to try to get rid of a partner in a horrendous way.

"He's in Switzerland," Kristen said.

"Then he could be out of cell range?"

"In Zurich?" Kristen's thumbs flew across her screen. "His secretary says he hasn't been at his hotel for two days."

"Do you want me to have someone look into whether or not he's come back to the States?"

She lowered the phone. "You can do that?"

"I can't, but I can get another agency to do it."

He called Callahan. Within fifteen minutes, they knew that Stephen Lang had not returned to the US. As far as anyone knew, he was still in Switzerland and merely out of cell range. But a lack of contact for two days raised suspicions.

The way Kristen rotated from reading files on her computer, to pacing the house, or start-ing back to the coffee table every time her phone pinged, then away again suggested to Nick she was worried.

In the middle of the afternoon, he made cof-fee and raided Gina's stash of cookies, then urged Kristen to sit and have a break. "Your feet must hurt."

"A little." She flopped onto a chair. "I see nothing significant in the files on my laptop. I should go to my office and look through files there. Not that I know how that will help. It would take weeks to eliminate anyone with a grudge or whatever is motivating this."

As if on cue, Kristen's cell phone rang. Both of them jumped and turned toward the device in its shiny red case.

Unknown Caller

Hand visibly shaking, Kristen reached for the phone.

FIVE

Kristen clicked the answer button, but when she opened her mouth to say hello, nothing came out. Part of her brain hoped a robotic voice or a prerecorded message would begin to play signaling a sales call of some kind or just a scammer.

Then Nick slipped the phone from her nerveless fingers and tilted it so that speaker mode toggled to on. The action gave Kristen the moment she needed to gather her wits and croak out, "Who...is this?"

"Listen, as I'm only saying this once." The voice sounded like a robocaller, mechanical and nearly flat in tone.

The inhuman voice continued with a time and location for the exchange. Kristen forced her brain to concentrate, to remember every detail. She knew the marshals were recording the call so they would know, but she didn't have that luxury. If she was going to go, whether they wanted her there or not—which of course they did not—she had to pay attention and forget nothing.

"You better have all that," the voice said.

"Wait," Kristen tried to interject.

That bloodcurdling scream sounded across the ether as it had the night before, and the call ended.

Kristen thought she was going to be sick.

Nick laid the phone on the table and touched her hand. "Deep breath, Kristen. That was prerecorded."

"All of it?"

"All of it. That was a computer reading everything."

"But the scream?"

Not her mother. Her mother wouldn't scream. Would she?

"As easily copied from a horror movie as real." Nick gave her an encouraging smile. "We'll have your mother back in a few hours."

"How without me?"

"I can't tell you that."

"Can't? Won't? Or you don't know?" She met his gaze with a challenging one of her own.

"I don't know exactly, but there are methods—"

"Which often fail."

"Nothing is foolproof."

"Letting me go so we can find out what they want—I mean, why they want me—is fool-proof."

"No one would agree to that, Kristen. Besides the fact you're a civilian, these men don't play by rules. They might keep or even kill both of you."

Before Kristen came up with an argument for that one, Nick's phone rang. He stood as he answered it, and headed for the front door, taking her phone with him.

Despite the chill at which Sean and Gina kept their house, Kristen grew hot all over. She wasn't sure if it was the way Nick dismissed her usefulness by pointing out her civilian status, as though civilians didn't count, or how he picked up her phone when he left for a private conversation. She only knew she was angry more than scared. These men had terrorized her and run her off the road. They had taken and possibly hurt her mother because they wanted something from Kristen. They had tried to kidnap her. The police and marshals had lost the one man who might have given them answers. Yet she was not supposed to be involved.

Somehow, she was going to be there tonight to make sure her mom was freed. More, she was going to ensure she learned why these men were after her so the marshals would know how to stop them. She knew she was in danger. She didn't think they wanted to kill her, at least not yet. If they only wanted her dead, they would have managed that too easily on the side of the expressway. They might want information she couldn't give them either literally or ethically. What would happen to her, she didn't know. But surely she could figure out something, some way to elude them. She was intelligent. She graduated at the top of her class from the University of Chicago.

Through the front window, she noticed that Nick had walked off the porch to talk. So he wanted to make sure she didn't overhear. That action added fuel to her fire to not cooperate with the Marshals Service or any other law enforcement agency involved. She didn't like being treated like a child who had to be kept in the dark about the issues that truly mattered.

Too often, her parents had done that. She'd learned of her mother's nomination to the federal bench from the newspaper, not her mother. She had been fourteen and Mom thought her too young to worry about the process. Mom's way of protecting Kristen.

Mom and Dad always tried to protect her. They had purchased a condo for her as a graduation gift, even though neither approved of her choice of careers. But they made sure it was in the suburbs not far from their house, though they knew she wanted to live in the city where her commute would be shorter and she could walk to restaurants and the grocery store. The first time Mom was threatened, Kristen had been dragged into the situation, grabbed out of class by marshals and locked in a safehouse, terrified and told too little until the threat was over. The second time, she knew nothing until the incident had passed.

And Mom had protected her the day before from something. Kristen knew Mom had been keeping something to herself, had been too quick to notice the SUV and jump to the conclusion it was up to no good. If she had told Kristen, maybe matters would have turned out differently.

Even allowing the men to take her and not Kristen had been a form of protection. The greatest form of protection.

Restless, Kristen rose and opened the front door. Behind her, Sean's office door opened. In front of her and in the planter-strewn courtyard between the carriage house and the apartment building, Nick looked up.

Kristen set her hands on her hips. "I'd like my phone back so I can call my dad again."

She wanted to leave him a voice mail if nothing else, to let him know what she intended to do. Just in case something went wrong. He needed to know. Kristen wasn't sure he deserved to know, going off the grid as he apparently had. At least she presumed he had disappeared voluntarily. Surely these kidnappers hadn't found him in Switzerland.

Another worry she did not need. She had to believe he, at least, was safe.

Nick said something into his phone she couldn't quite hear, then returned it to his pocket before he climbed the porch steps. "We'll get you another phone."

"But all my numbers are in that one you took away from me."

"I know. It's terrible how we don't know anything without our phones anymore." Nick grinned.

Kristen looked away so her foolish female side didn't respond to the charm of that grin.

"I can let you copy all the numbers." Nick drew out her phone, though he didn't give it to her. "Will that help?"

"I guess it'll have to."

She must appear to cooperate.

"I'm sure Sean can give you some paper and a pencil." Nick kept coming toward her, so Kristen had to step out of the doorway and let him pass. Except he didn't cross the threshold.

"After you, madam." He gave her a little bow.

"Do you think I'm going to run out the door if you go first?" Kristen made herself laugh. "You could probably catch me in five minutes or less."

"Probably, but I'd rather not have to try."

Kristen shrugged and strolled into the house. Sean was making coffee in the kitchen. "There's paper and pencils on my desk, Kristen. Help yourself."

"You have about a half hour to copy all the names you want," Nick said as he locked the front door. "Someone will be here to pick you up then."

"Pick me up?" Kristen spun around halfway across the dining room. "Pick me up for what?"

"In the light of this phone call, we are placing you in protective custody until Her Honor is released."

"But I thought…tomorrow…" Kristen's mind raced.

She had counted on being able to get away tonight, elude Nick in the dark. Now she would have to find a way to do so in the daylight, not as easy. Not easy at all. Probably impossible without a ruse.

She would find one.

"Then let me get that paper." As though she wasn't in the least bothered by the protective custody idea, she continued to the office, where she located paper and pencils. The room was small but efficiently set up with a desk with a monitor, and smaller tables containing a printer and other monitors. One of those monitors showed a split-screen view of the exterior of the carriage house. Kristen recognized the views—outside the front door. Outside the dining room, outside her bedroom. None outside the bathroom. Turning away from the screens, she headed for the dining room to spread the paper and pencils out on the table.

Nick offered her coffee, fetched them each a cup, then joined her at the table. He laid her phone between them. More texts from friends filled the screen. No missed calls. Nothing from her father.

Kristen unlocked the phone and scrolled through her contacts. Her parents' and boss's numbers. Her closest friends'. Who else? Her pastor's number, maybe? Why not.

The contacts copied, she folded the half sheet and slipped it into the pocket of her jeans.

"That's all?" Nick asked.

Kristen shrugged. "All I should need for the next day or two."

"But we'll need your phone for evidence, you know."

She hadn't thought of that—that keeping her phone would be as good as permanent.

"I think the rest should be in the cloud and I can transfer them when I get a new phone." She made herself smile. "I know it's on a giant server somewhere, but I like thinking about a fluffy white cloud in the sky holding all my pictures and numbers and appointments. And one day it'll get too heavy and dark and all those pictures and numbers will just tumble from the sky."

Nick looked bemused.

Kristen laughed for real this time and rose. "I'm really not going nuts, Deputy Marshal Sandoval. Just a little stir-crazy." She grimaced. "And it's going to be worse in—" she made air quotes "—protective custody. And if they're coming to take me away soon, I better make sure all my stuff is together."

She left Nick at the table and retreated to the guest room. Her stuff was still together. All she could take with her was her purse, which was fortunately a fairly large cross-body satchel. She stuffed some toiletries inside along with a few other necessities, then slipped into the bathroom.

The carriage house had been built at least a hundred years ago and had obviously not included two bathrooms en suite. Probably not even one. Either Sean and Gina or previous owners had added such luxuries. But they had kept the original exterior of the old building, which meant the bathroom boasted a window on one wall that could be opened. Not a large window, but big enough for Kristen to wriggle through. The problem lay in the drop to the ground. The carriage house was built over a basement only half cut into the ground. That made the drop a minimum of ten feet. She could dangle from her hands and fall, but if she landed incorrectly, she could twist an ankle or worse. Not to mention the impact of landing on her still-sore feet.

She would do it. She had to get away before she was locked into some prison, even if it was a comfortable house or hotel room, her every move guarded for her own good.

Time was wasting. Shortly, Nick would be knocking on the door. Worse, if a female deputy marshal showed up, they might break into the bathroom to see what was taking Kristen so long.

Making sure her purse was tightly zipped, she dropped it into the bushes outside the window. Those plants would help break her own fall. She hated the idea of crushing them, but they would grow back. This was only June. Listening for anyone coming into the bedroom, Kristen climbed onto the vanity, then stepped on top of the tank. She practically had to manage a handstand to go out feetfirst, but with her hands braced on the vanity, her torso twisted, she got one leg and then the other over the sill. Immediately, gravity took over and she began to slide. For a heartbeat, she feared she would crash to the ground in an uncontrolled descent. A cry rose in her throat. She clamped her mouth shut to keep any sound inside and flung out her hands to catch the edge of the sill.

Her fall stopped with an abruptness that wrenched her shoulders. She gasped with pain. One of her sneakers, loosely tied so she could keep her feet bandaged, fell into the shrubbery beside her purse.

She had underestimated the ten-foot fall. Surely, it must have been at least fifteen or twenty. She was going to break something for sure. Without the upper body strength to drag herself back inside the window, and the idea of being locked up while her mother suffered or worse driving her on, Kristen let go.

She landed with a thud and crackle of breaking branches. For several minutes, she huddled in a heap of arms and legs, assessing potential damage to her person and tried to breathe like normal, not like someone who had just run a marathon.

Certain everything was where it should be, she retrieved her shoe and tied it on, grabbed her purse and began to creep along the base of the house where the camera angle wouldn't pick up her movements unless someone shifted them. Until Nick or Sean realized she had escaped, they wouldn't move those cameras.

At the front of the house, she'd have to cross the open courtyard. She might be seen at that point if anyone was watching the cameras. She might get caught if the deputy marshals sent to collect her arrived as she exited the gate.

She would certainly be caught if she remained still.

At the front corner of the house, she took a deep breath and sprinted to the gangway. The dimness between the two apartment buildings, not more than five feet apart, swallowed her up. There were possibly more cameras here. Couldn't be helped now. She just kept going. The gate was locked. She tapped in the code she had memorized watching Sean and Nick type it, hoping neither had changed it, and exited.

The street with cars lining both sides lay ahead of her, quiet in the weekday afternoon. She ran across, then used the opposite line of vehicles as cover to the end of the block. Another less busy street, then Lincoln Avenue, which was never quiet. And she could see the "L" station two blocks away. Just two blocks away, and no one had shouted her name yet. No feet pounded after her.

So as not to draw attention to herself, she strolled with everyone else walking dogs, going for an afternoon caffeine pick-me-up, enjoying the lovely summer day.

She reached the station still without anyone following her that she noticed. A swipe of her CTA card allowed her through the turnstile and up the steps. She took the elevator to spare her feet, for speed, for concealment. On the platform, the board said a train was due in three minutes. Only three minutes until she would board the elevated train and become nearly impossible to catch.

"Two minutes until the arrival of a train bound for The Loop," an inhuman female voice announced over the loudspeaker.

Kristen glanced over the waist-high railing that was the only barricade between the platform and the ground more than twenty feet below.

And saw Nick Sandoval headed straight for the station entrance.

With the rumble of the oncoming train fast approaching, Nick vaulted the gate and charged for the steps. If no one stopped him, he would catch the train and prevent it from leaving the station in the event the woman he had seen enter the building moments ahead of him was Kristen.

"Halt right there, young man." Of course someone held him up—the station manager. He had the lined face of an older man, but the physique of someone who worked out on a regular basis.

Nick doubted he would be able to push past this gentleman without causing trouble he didn't want.

"Deputy US Marshal Nicholas Sandoval." Nick held out his credentials.

Above him, the train rattled into the station, the two-tone door chime sounding, the announcer's voice declaring the name of the station.

"There's a person I need to stop from getting on that train." Nick sighed as the train's rumble roared down the stairwell.

"L" trains didn't remain in the station for long.

"*Needed* to stop from getting on that train," Nick corrected himself. "Can we stop it before it gets to the next station?"

"I can try, but the stations are close together here and we only got a minute." The station manager walked and talked at the same time, heading for his booth.

But he had to take out his keys and unlock the gate, and then he had to unlock the door. Once inside, he called someone, who insisted, apparently at a manager's request, for Nick's credentials again, to know his badge number to verify Nick truly was with the Marshals Service. By the time the information got through, the train had left the next station only half a mile down the track.

"But we got it stopped at the next one," the station manager said.

"Thank you." Pocketing his credentials, Nick raced back to Gina's house to retrieve his car, talking to his office the whole way. He and the two marshals sent to collect Kristen Lang met at the station, but Kristen wasn't among the restless and annoyed passengers. She had either not been on the train at all or had gotten off at the next station. She could be anywhere in the transit system or on foot. With time, they could get her transit records and follow her movements if she was using a registered transit card. He suspected she must be. She hadn't had time to purchase a short-term ticket.

But that would take too long. She could hop in a taxi or rent a car before they knew where she was headed.

Except Nick did know where she was headed later that day.

"How did you lose her?" one of Nick's co-workers asked, meeting him back at the carriage house.

"She went out the bathroom window." Nick met the female marshal's gaze. "I didn't think Kristen would fit through that window or want to risk the drop to the ground from that height. It's about twelve feet."

"She wanted free in a bad way." The female deputy marshal held out her hand. "I'm Stephanie Kelly and this is Marcos Segovia. You're Sandoval, I presume."

"You presume right." Nick speared his fingers through his hair, knowing it would now be standing on end. "I should have guessed she was up to something when she was so calm about you two coming to take her to a safe house."

"The question now is how do we find her?" Segovia said.

"I wish that wasn't easy." Nick climbed the porch steps, the other two marshals behind him.

"How?" Segovia asked.

"She's going to meet her mother's kidnappers." Nick rang the doorbell.

Sean arrived to open it immediately. "Didn't catch up with her?"

Nick didn't answer the obvious.

Sean stepped back so they could all enter.

"I'm sorry. I didn't put cameras outside the bathroom window. It just seemed wrong, and that window is pretty small and high up."

"Not small and high up enough," Kelly said. "Do you want to call the office or should I, Sandoval?"

"I already have. I'm waiting for Callahan to call me back."

Not waiting with any anticipation. As his six-year-old nephew would say, *You're in big trouble.*

All he had to do was watch over one quiet and anxious female, to keep her safe from harm, and he had let her go.

He had failed again to protect someone with whom God had trusted him.

"She's going to be at the exchange point tonight," Nick said.

His phone rang, and he repeated the words to his boss.

Callahan said a great deal about Nick losing another lady he was supposed to keep safe. Even if Michele hadn't officially been Nick's responsibility, her death surely had been, no matter what others tried to tell him. Callahan, Nick's boss and Michele's father, made disparaging comments at least once a week, solidifying Nick's personal conviction about his incompetence as a marshal.

He should be given no more responsibility than watching the metal detectors in the courthouse.

"You aren't competent enough to handle more than watching the metal detectors in the courthouse," Callahan echoed Nick's thoughts, "in someplace like Franklin, Tennessee, or maybe Brownsville, Texas."

"Yes, sir." Nick's neck and ears scorched.

His colleagues and brother-in-law might not be able to hear Callahan, but they were laughing at his discomfort.

"We can catch up with her tonight if we don't before then." Nick tried to defuse his boss's temper.

"Does she have her phone?" Callahan asked. "We can triangulate it."

"No, sir, I have it."

Nick wanted to sink into Sean and Gina's basement.

He remembered how. She had written down all those names and numbers to put into a new phone, a burner phone she could buy in a hundred different places in the city.

"Credit cards?" Nick asked.

"She used an ATM at Halsted and Clybourn," Callahan said.

So she had cash to buy a burner phone and hire a taxi from any street corner, which would be less traceable than using a car service from an app that required a credit card.

Aware of three pairs of eyes upon him, Nick asked, "What steps would you like me to take now, sir?"

"I want you here immediately." Callahan's tone was uncompromising. "Maybe when you're explaining how you lost a civilian, you'll figure out something about how we can stop her from reaching the rendezvous site and messing up our operation."

"Yes, sir." Nick signed off and shrugged. "I'm off to take my punishment like a man." He snatched his jacket on the way to the door.

"Sandoval?" Kelly followed him, blocking his path of egress. "Doesn't this all seem suspicious to you?"

"All what? The kidnapping of the judge or Kristen escaping?"

Nick guessed where his coworker was going—the same way as the media. Nick had been able to dismiss the idea of Kristen's involvement without hesitation that morning, but right then, he wasn't as sure of her innocence as he had been a few hours ago.

"She's behaved with a pretty cool and calculating head for a civilian whose mother was just kidnapped," Stephanie Kelly said. "Do you think she's involved?"

Nick opened his mouth to deny the possibility, but doubts niggling at his brain kept him from the negative he wished to speak. "I think she's determined to make up for her mother getting kidnapped while preventing those men from taking her."

"She can't be doing that." Segovia's face paled. "She'll get herself and law enforcement killed, if these men are inclined to be that violent."

"When you're looking at decades in prison," Kelly said, "most men are willing to kill to escape it."

"And Kristen was willing to risk a great deal to keep from being locked up in a safehouse." Nick still sought for an excuse other than guilt to cover her behavior.

"We have no reason to believe she's involved," was all he knew to say.

It was the simple truth.

"We don't know why these men would want her instead of her mother, either," Kelly reminded them.

"Seems to me," Marcos said, "the judge is more important than her daughter any day."

"She's a victim's advocate. Maybe she helped the wrong person." Nick turned sideways to edge around Kelly. "I'd better go face the music."

"Like your funeral dirge." Marcos grinned.

Nick grimaced, called a thank-you to Sean and headed for his car. Traffic was going to be terrible heading into The Loop. It wasn't terrible enough. He knew what was coming—he was off the case. He didn't need the aggravation of crawling along Lake Shore Drive with the beauty of the blue lake taunting him against the foreground of snarled traffic to hear his boss yell at him in person.

But yelled at in person was what he got when he finally reached the office.

"Your brother-in-law's house is like a fortress, you told me—" Callahan began without so much as a hello, "—cameras everywhere."

"It is. They are." Nick stood in the doorway, not having been invited in farther.

"And after you let that one kidnapper go yester—"

"Excuse me, sir, but my job is to protect the judge and her family, and that was what I was doing. The cops are the ones who—"

"And you failed to protect the judge and her family." Callahan was close to shouting. Although the other office doors were closed, Nick didn't doubt for a moment ears were pressed to the other sides of the panels to listen.

Nick closed his eyes, expecting to see Michele's sweet and delicate face. Instead, an image of Kristen with her strong-boned features, deep-blue eyes and yards of blond hair blazed across the insides of his eyelids. Kristen on her own and prepared to meet monsters with only herself as a bargaining tool.

"Please, sir—" Nick began to explain why he believed Kristen ran. "Kristen would rather—"

"Be on her own than in our protection?" Callahan cut in.

"Yes, sir. She is tired of standing by doing nothing after her mother stopped those men from taking her. She feels guilty and wants to be involved—"

"You got to know her well." Callahan's voice held a sneer.

"I thought I was supposed to, sir." Nick spoke with exaggerated calm. "She wants—however mistakenly—to meet these men."

"Because she's involved?" Callahan asked.

"With all due respect, sir, why would she be involved with her own mother's kidnapping?"

"To get attention. To get money out of her parents. Because she's angry with them. There's a dozen reasons why a daughter might do something like this."

"But—" Nick stopped, unable to find a single argument.

He didn't know Kristen that well. He could only go on his instincts that said she wasn't involved in any criminal manner.

Yet the media had started it, perhaps with a little help from Callahan, Nick realized, and now the Marshals Service and probably others had continued the idea that Kristen was part of the abduction.

"If she's involved," Nick asked, "why would these men offer to release Her Honor in an exchange?"

"To make Kristen look innocent," Callahan suggested.

"That's a weak reason, sir."

"We can't overlook the circumstances that point to Kristen's involvement, including her running off today."

"But—"

"Go home," Callahan ordered. "Report to the courthouse tomorrow."

"Yes, sir." Though he flinched as if each word were a blow, Nick knew better than to argue.

In silence, he left the doorway, exited the building. Moments later, he was headed to his apartment in Old Town. It was small, a mere studio flat, but big enough for his needs since he was rarely there. He could take the "L" or even walk to work if he liked. He only drove his car on the days he headed to the suburbs to have dinner with one of his numerous family members who had taken upon themselves the task of feeding him, the only unmarried sibling.

This afternoon, the apartment looked no larger than a shoe box, too high off the ground, too stagnant in its recirculated air-conditioned air. He wanted the freshness of the woods, of the breeze off the lake.

He wanted to find Kristen.

He was ordered to begin work at the courthouse as usual the next day. But Kristen was at large that night. Finding her before the rendezvous was going to be nearly impossible, but just maybe he could stop her right at the rendezvous.

He knew Callahan would have something similar in play, but maybe she would listen to Nick. He thought they were building some sort of rapport, a hint of trust.

"Except she ran away from you," he reminded himself aloud.

What he was about to do could get him fired. No, it would get him fired if Kristen was involved in the abduction and not a victim. Nick didn't think she was part of these men's scheme, but everyone else did, so he had to stop her before she tangled herself worse than she already had. Maybe if he could rescue her, he would make up for failing to rescue Michele.

Knowing his livelihood—the career he had

planned for as far back as he could remember—was on the line, he gathered some things together and made his plans to stop Kristen at the rendezvous, if not before.

SIX

Kristen waited out the afternoon in the public library mere blocks from the courthouse. She figured no one would find her there, or even think to look for her anywhere in The Loop. With multiple floors and numerous nooks and crannies, the library proved a quiet and safe refuge from anyone wanting to harm her, which included the US Marshals Service.

She considered it harm, even if they considered it her safety. They wanted to lock her away like she was the criminal. For all she knew, the media was right and someone high up in the service did believe she was a criminal, that she had helped kidnap her mother.

But getting away from pursuit had been easy. Easier than she'd expected—so easy that finding her might be simple as well.

After seeing Nick approaching the "L" station, she'd hopped on the train, then exited at the next station and descended to street level to catch a bus. Stopping trains wouldn't take much effort for law enforcement. Buses weren't so easy. They had to figure out which one she took, so she switched buses three times, stopping along the way to get cash from an ATM and buy a burner phone. Her trip downtown took her nearly two hours with all the stops and switches, but she was still free.

She needed a plan for getting her mother free.

"Too little to go on." She murmured the words to the purse-sized notebook open on the table before her. She tapped the eraser of her pencil on the lined page. "Too little."

A couple other patrons glanced her way, then quickly looked somewhere else. They would think she was just another odd person spending her time in a public place.

She needed to not act too oddly. Oddity drew attention and that was the last thing she wanted.

And thinking of attention, she needed to cover her hair. She could do nothing about her height, but her height plus her long, pale blond hair drew attention.

She ducked into a discount store and bought a baseball cap and hair bands. Braided, her hair wasn't as noticeable, especially beneath the cap. She considered sunglasses, but not for the evening. But she did buy a hoodie. June nights could still be chilly outside the city or by the lake.

Now to get out of the city.

Afraid the two stations for the commuter rails would be watched, Kristen coughed up the money to take a taxi she merely flagged down on the street. With cash for payment, no record of who she was or where she had gotten on or off would be connected to her name or her bank or credit card accounts.

The ride north took forever. Kristen employed all her willpower not to look behind her, check the back window to see if anyone followed. Of course they didn't. No one knew where she was.

They would know where she was going, though. She didn't doubt it for a minute. Some sort of law enforcement would wait for her, would try to stop her from meeting her mother's kidnappers. Nick? Maybe. She wondered if he had gotten into trouble for letting her slip away. That was the problem with going off on her own—others could get hurt in the process. She hoped her actions didn't damage his career, or at least not beyond repair. He had merely been following orders when he intended to turn her over to other marshals for confinement. "And I was only doing what I needed to for my mother's sake."

"Beg pardon?" the driver asked.

"Nothing. Just thinking aloud." She smiled. "I talk to myself sometimes."

"It's okay, just don't answer." The driver laughed as though he had made a great joke.

Kristen forced herself to smile in acknowledgment of his attempt at humor. Then she turned her attention to her purse, removing things she could tuck into her clothing in the event the pocketbook was taken from her or she had to abandon it. The sheet with phone numbers. The burner phone. The rest of her cash… That task done, she faced the window, seeking the correct exit for the nature preserve along the Des Plaines River.

"There." She tapped the side window.

"You sure?" The driver, who looked like he'd been at the job of ferrying people around for half a century, gave her a concerned glance in the rearview mirror. "They close soon."

"I know. I'm meeting someone who is… um…working here." She hoped that wasn't too much of a fib.

It was, in a sick way, the truth. The kidnappers were working there, and she intended to meet them.

Law enforcement could enter the park after closing hours, but she, a mere civilian, could not. She had to find her way in and hide until the rendezvous time. So did the kidnappers. So might law enforcement, figuring she and the men who had taken her mother would be there.

For a moment, as she paid the driver, she panicked over the thought the park might be closed already. The marshals might have ordered it to stop the kidnappers from using the area. Yet if they did that, they wouldn't have a chance of getting the judge back.

If they ever had a chance of getting her back.

Kristen was about to ask the driver to wait in the event she couldn't get into the park by any conventional means, when she spied three cars exiting. Two SUVs and a minivan, to be specific. All of them teemed with children and women who were probably their moms. It looked like the end of an elementary school picnic and nature hike. The park possessed many activities for children, Kristen remembered from her own childhood. She had gone there with her Sunday school class, the only child without some relative present in the form of a mom or dad, a cousin or sibling. She had gotten stuck in a bathroom stall with a lock that refused to budge. With no one specifically looking out for her, she had been there for half an hour before someone noticed her absence.

She hadn't thought of that incident in years. Now, watching the vehicles full of children and adults cruise past her, memories of that day, at least eighteen years earlier, flashed through her mind, and her breath snagged in her throat. Her heart began to race.

No, no, no, no, no, she would not have a panic attack now. She needed to remain calm, clearheaded, strong.

She slipped from the cab and took a deep breath of sweet-smelling air. This was as close to country air as she ever got. She couldn't remember the last time she spent any time in nature.

She was going to spend some time now.

Head down in the event the reserve shone cameras on the entrance, she entered the grounds. The river was her goal. She could find a place to hide and wait by there. It wasn't far. She knew the way. She had printed off a map in the library.

Striding with purpose, the best way not to get stopped, she headed down the trail. She smelled the coolness of water, the freshness of greenery. Birds sang their joy in the clarity of the late afternoon, drowning the sound of her footfalls on the path and the splashing of water.

She had escaped from Nick and the marshals. But she hadn't taken a moment to think and pray about the danger of what she was doing. She might have just given up the safe confinement of the marshal's safehouse for the treacherous captivity of ruthless kidnappers. Yet she didn't know how else she could save her mother.

Nick sprinted across the landscape toward the tall woman with a baseball cap minimizing the shine of her hair.

She rounded a bend in the path.

Nick put on a burst of speed and caught up with her. Though always reluctant to touch a woman without permission, he caught hold of her arm, compelling her to pause.

"Kristen, you can't do this."

She wrenched her arm free and faced him. "You weren't supposed to find me."

"It's my job."

"Pretend you couldn't find me."

"I can't do that. You have to come back with me, not go meeting up with criminals."

"I have to. Don't you understand?"

"No." Nick set his hands on his hips. "I don't understand why you want to put yourself in harm's way when we have a plan in place to get your mother released."

"I'm sure you do. But will it bring an end to whatever these men want?"

"If—" Nick caught himself and corrected, "When we catch them we will."

"And that *if.* If you don't, or if one gets away, or if there are more, when will this end for me?"

Nick held her gaze. "Tonight, if you don't interfere."

"Is that a threat?" She held his gaze with her eyes wide and bluer than the sky.

And doing something odd to his middle. Softening it like a square of baking chocolate he'd seen his mother liquefy in a pan.

He took a step back as though the action could return his core to its solid state. "I don't threaten civilians. I was merely warning you that you can be locked up, charged with interference, or you could be hurt if those men want to harm you."

"They don't want to harm me yet. That was obvious when they didn't just do so at the accident site. They want something from me."

"And you have no idea what?"

Nick studied her face, seeking a hint she wasn't telling the truth when she answered.

"I have no idea." Suddenly her shoulders sagged and she leaned against a tree, arms crossed at her waist. "I don't know." She closed her eyes. "I've looked through the few files on my computer, and I've had hours to think about everyone I've worked with whom I can remember, and nothing comes to me. Or maybe it's more like too much comes to me. I've helped wives get away from abusive spouses, and more than you might think were from well-off families. Same with some kids I've helped. And then we have assault victims…" She trailed off and opened her eyes. "I just don't know. I won't ever know if I don't confront these men."

"Let law enforcement catch them and then find out."

Nick didn't want to so much as think about her face-to-face with men who would dare kidnap a federal judge, even if they were just using her to get to her daughter instead.

"And you can guarantee whoever shows up tonight are the only men after me?"

"We can never guarantee anything of the kind. I won't lie to you."

"And what will you all do? Have a female marshal or special agent pretend to be me and identify herself after Mom is free?"

"I don't know the plan," Nick admitted.

Her eyes widened. "You're not a part of the operation after babysitting me for the last day?"

"I let you escape." Nick looked away, his ears growing hot. "My boss sent me home."

"I'm so sorry." She sounded sincere. "I was afraid this might interfere with your career."

Nick shrugged. "It happens. Callahan doesn't

like me much, so he's always looking for excuses to keep me out of important tasks."

"Why doesn't he—" She stopped.

Nick felt how stiff his facial muscles had grown and guessed why she hadn't completed the question as to why Callahan didn't like the youngest deputy marshal under his command.

"We need to get out of here." Nick changed the topic. "Whatever is going down here, we will get in the way."

"So you haven't listened to me at all." With a sigh, Kristen turned toward the head of the trail, toward the park entrance.

Nick fell into step beside her. "I've listened. I just happen to disagree with your reasoning. You work with the victims of crimes, not the criminals themselves." He let out a rueful laugh. "I haven't dealt much with criminals other than making sure they get to the right courthouse at the right time."

But he'd been trained to handle crises, trained to watch and listen and take in his environment. At that moment, his environment felt off and he couldn't place why. Birds still sang in the trees and swooped overhead, though they seemed fewer than they had a few minutes ago. No car doors slammed, and no parents called to children to get into vehicles. The park was deserted, empty of employees and visitors alike.

Except for the quieter birds.

His and Kristen's presence could have disturbed the birds into toning down their singing. Yet they had been carrying on just fine when he followed her down the path toward the river.

The river.

He heard it then, the whine of an outboard motor on the water. Not unusual. Motor craft were allowed on the Des Plaines, but mostly people used canoes and rowboats because of a scarcity of boat launches. So in the quiet of the park after hours, the motor sounded as annoying as a single mosquito in the dead of night. Again, nothing to worry about. The river wasn't closed to traffic. Daylight was still strong. But something was off.

Why wasn't the river closed? If law enforcement intended to catch the kidnappers, surely they would have checkpoints on the river as well as the land.

Too early. That was it. The rendezvous wasn't for another four hours and no one wished to tip their hand too much ahead of time. He was worrying for nothing. Still, he wanted to get Kristen out of the park and to safety as quickly as possible.

He touched her elbow with the tips of his fingers. "Let me take you back. You'll only have to be under guard for one night."

And Callahan would forgive some of Nick's shortcomings if he returned Kristen to the marshals' custody.

She didn't flinch away from his touch. She didn't argue. In fact, she nodded and kept walking toward the road.

"They're not going to hurt Her Honor, you know." Nick offered the little comfort he could. "That would be beyond foolish."

She snorted. "And criminals are never beyond foolish?"

Nick laughed. "You're right about that. But, seriously, this will all work out just fine."

Behind them, the whine of the outboard motor stopped. Someone with mechanical trouble or simply deciding to halt in midstream. Nothing more.

Ahead of Nick, Kristen tilted her head. She kept walking, though.

He heaved a sigh of relief, glad she had decided to go along with him, with what the Marshals Service wanted. This was for the best. This was how she would remain safe.

They reached his car, parked along the road. The top was down on such a beautiful day. In a hurry to look for Kristen, Nick hadn't raised the roof before exiting the vehicle and hadn't bothered to lock it, a pointless exercise with the car exposed to the world. He still opened the door for Kristen. She slid into the seat and caught hold of the door to close it herself before he could do it for her. Letting her have her moment of independence, he shrugged and walked around the hood toward the driver's side. He had barely shut his door before a semi roared up the road like some mammoth bearing down on a fox. Nick turned his head to ensure the truck didn't remove his side mirror.

And in those moments, when the towering wheels of the tractor-trailer loomed beside him, Kristen pushed her door open and was out of the car and racing toward the river.

SEVEN

She might have bruised and scratched feet, but Kristen Lang was a runner. By the time Nick was able to scramble from his vehicle and dash after her, she was almost at the river.

"Kristen, stop," he shouted several times.

She continued to sprint around a curve, between trees, out of his sight. Though he couldn't see her, he heard her, the crunch of gravel beneath her sneakers, the crackle of branches she brushed past. Then nothing.

Nick halted, listening. The woods were quiet. Too quiet. The birds had fallen nearly silent. Kristen no longer sprinted along the path, or she had figured out how to run without making a sound—an impossible feat.

Something was wrong. Nick didn't need to see what had happened ahead of him to know trouble had fallen on Kristen. On Kristen and, by association, on him.

Part of him thought he should get out of earshot of the river and call for help. Help, however, would probably take too long to get there, especially if he turned back and crept away as quietly as he could manage.

He did the next best thing and texted his boss. KLang at rendezvous site. Maybe trouble.

He waited for a response. None came. He texted again. Advise course of action. She won't come with me.

The response came at last. Make her.

Great. He was to forcibly remove Kristen from the park. How did Callahan propose he do that? He didn't have handcuffs, moving her at gunpoint seemed ridiculous overkill, and he could hardly pick her up and toss her over his shoulder.

Though he hadn't minded carrying her the night before when her feet were bleeding.

He shoved that memory aside. Now was not a time to think about his attraction to a lady he scarcely knew.

Will do my best. He had barely hit Send when he heard the whine of the outboard motor.

The outboard. A boat. A wide-open river.

Nick started to run. So what if he sounded like a heard of cattle charging across the prairie? He knew how to put two and two together and jump to an all too likely conclusion.

Kristen's running stopped. Silence. Then the starting of the motorboat.

He prayed he was wrong. She was merely crouching behind bushes watching and waiting. The motorboat had started up because the passengers wanted to be on their way.

He broke through the trees to see the river flowing slow and smooth before him. Yards of river between the bank and the boat. And in the boat, a man twice her size crowded beside her, sat Kristen.

Nick didn't think further than tossing his cell phone and gun onto the riverbank and kicking off his shoes. Then he dove into the river and began to swim. He was a strong swimmer, but he was swimming in a race against a motorized boat. If the men in the craft, the one driving and the one seeming to guard Kristen, looked back, they would see him. They could run him down, tear him up with the blades of the motor, swamp him with their wake.

He stayed below the surface as much as he dared. The water was murky. Fortunately, the current was slow on this prairie river through flat land. And they were moving downstream with that current.

Still, he would never catch them. Strong swimmer or not, the motor pulled the boat farther and farther ahead of Nick.

Until he noticed the tone of the engine change from the high whine of speed, to the putt-putt-putt of a boat slowing.

He lifted his head from the water in time to see the boat turning toward him, coming straight at him.

He dove deep, reaching for the bottom of the river. Water magnified the motor to a roar above him. He saw the shadow of the craft slip over him, then swing around for another pass.

He had to surface. He couldn't hold his breath any longer. If he came up at the wrong place and time, the boat could plow him under, injure him, even kill him.

Maybe they would move on. They had what—who—they wanted.

Kristen captive in their boat.

With Kristen captured, they wouldn't let Nick, a deputy U.S. marshal, go. Killing him was their intent.

He would drown and do the job for them if he didn't surface. Attempting to swim toward the bank, more out of the boat's trajectory, he pushed himself to the surface and gasped for air. Before he had inhaled a lungful of oxygen, the driver of the boat saw him and drove straight at him. For a heartbeat, Nick looked into the man's eyes, saw the murderous intent.

Then Nick dove. The water rocked him with the boat passing too close overhead.

Passing over and stopping, motor whining to a painful pitch before dying altogether.

Nick surfaced again, treading water as he saw the boat trapped in a tangle of brush along the bank. Intent on running Nick down, the driver had plowed the prow right into the soft bank.

Under other circumstances, Nick would have laughed. But he was cold and wet, his clothes beginning to feel like leaden weights on his arms and legs, and Kristen was in that boat.

All he could think to do was attempt to tip it over. Not that difficult. The boat was barely large enough for the two men and Kristen. In the ensuing scramble to not drown after he capsized the boat, he could grab Kristen and get them away.

He swam toward the craft and launched himself out of the water high enough to grasp the gunwale. The boat tilted, but not enough. The prow in the bank kept it from tipping.

Still holding the side with one hand, Nick reached the other hand toward Kristen, curled his fingers around her arm.

She started to lean toward him. Then suddenly she was down, wrenched from his hold to land on the bottom of the boat. Nick caught the gunwale with his freed hand to maintain his position. A mistake to stay. He should have shoved himself away and swum toward the bank, run for help. Marshals would certainly be arriving at the park any moment now. But he'd been too intent upon saving Kristen and now faced the round eye of a gun pointed at his face.

"Get in," the burly man growled.

"Nick, no." Kristen hurled herself between Nick and the pistol.

The burly man grabbed her shoulder and held the gun against her temple. "Get in," he repeated to Nick.

Nick climbed into the boat and kneeled on the bottom. "Now what?"

Kristen longed for the strength to pick him up and drop him back into the water. He had come after her. He shouldn't have come after her. He was ruining everything with his overblown sense of duty.

"You'll take a little ride with us."

"Seems to me, you're not riding anywhere." Tone scornful, Nick gestured toward the prow of the boat caught in the bank.

When he drew his hand back, he wrapped his arm around Kristen's waist, pulling her against him. She shivered, but not from the cold wetness of his clothes. The frisson ran far deeper than a mere chill of her skin.

Maybe annoyance? With his arm around her, he couldn't get away as easily if the men became distracted.

She pushed at his shoulder. He held on tighter. "I have a plan," he murmured.

But they weren't that careless. The man who had been piloting the boat was already using an oar to shove the craft away from the bank. Though the current wasn't strong, it seemed to be enough to help tug the boat free with the aid of the oar. In mere moments, they were adrift on the river. Then the motor coughed to life and they were flying along the river, past trees, open land and houses. All the while, the burly man held the pistol to Kristen's temple in a silent message for her and Nick not to move, not to speak.

But they weren't tied up. Surely she could find a way to get Nick freed, if they remained unbound. They couldn't remain on the river forever. It wasn't that long and had dams to interrupt the open river for watercraft.

They were on the water long enough to carry them miles from the park. He had wet clothes and no shoes. And surely any firearm and certainly his phone would have been destroyed in the water. Kristen's purse had been left behind.

They would be tracked as far as the river and no farther.

Nick had to get out of this. Somehow. If the men were going to kill her and not take her in exchange for her mother, Kristen needed to get out of this, too. Nick would find an opportunity. The assurance kept her calm.

The men nosed the boat into the bank again, this time not at random, a planned destination where two more men met them.

"Get out." The burly man with the gun seemed to be the only one who spoke, the only voice Kristen would be able to identify later if they got away, if these men were caught.

A gesture with the gun sent Nick over the side of the boat to half swim, half walk to the bank. Once he reached it, one of the men there dragged him onto dry land, then spun him around and bound his hands. His feet were free. He could run.

Kristen prayed he would, but of course he didn't, this modern knight errant. He waited for her to splash through the thigh-deep water and scramble up the muddy bank. On dry land, she stumbled along, feeling sick. Nick smiled at her, trying to reassure her. In response, her lower lip quivered.

"Walk," the burly man commanded.

They walked through brush and trees to a

road that didn't look traveled much or as if it got much attention. The blacktop was bubbled and cracked from the winter's ice expansion and contraction. But one vehicle sat on the side of the road—a cargo van. Of course it was a cargo van. It was even white.

"How cliché," Nick muttered.

Kristen swallowed hysterical laughter.

Nick's remark earned him a jab in the back that sent him staggering into the open rear door of the van. His cheekbone collided with the frame. Kristen caught her breath. At best, he would have a bruise. At worst, a black eye.

"Get them in," the burly man spoke to his cohort for the first time. "Secure them."

"Wait." Kristen grasped the edge of the door to the cargo bay and faced the men. "Where's my mother?"

"None of your business."

"Of course it's my business." Kristen glared at her captors. "You promised to free her if you got me, so you need to set her free."

"As if these men have honor," Nick said.

"I will think they do until they prove otherwise." Kristen's voice shook and she pressed her hands to her spasming middle, but she didn't flinch from the man with the gun.

"Tie them up." The burly guy's gravely voice held no emotion, no appreciation of the gift

Kristen had just bestowed upon him—a belief that he held a core of goodness.

The men trussed them up like chickens. Kristen knew Nick could have fought them, yet he didn't. For her sake. He let himself get captured for her sake. Orders from his boss to keep an eye on her no matter what? Or something...more important?

The doors shut. Darkness descended on the interior. Darkness and quiet, save for the rumble of the van's engine starting, the thud of other doors closing, the crunching of tires over uneven pavement.

The roughness of the road bounced Kristen off the side of the van, then into the middle. A thud and a grunt told her Nick suffered much the same discomfort.

"Try to brace yourself in a corner." He spoke to her.

The van careened around a bend and Kristen slid into him. "I'm sorry."

"No problem. Can you pull yourself up if you grab my shirt or arm?"

"I'll try." With a few "oophs" of discomfort, and a tear in Nick's shirt, she used her bound hands to haul herself upright against his shoulder.

"I'll try to scooch to the corner," she said.

"No, stay."

She stayed. She rested her head on his shoulder and loosed a long, shuddering sigh. "This is my fault. I should have listened to you."

"You wanted to help your mother."

"I needed to stop being the one everyone protects and do something for myself. I guess that's why—" She broke off to take another long breath and suppress a sob.

"Kristen." Nick's voice was low and smooth. "Are you all right?"

"I…don't…think…so." A gasping breath punctuated each word. "I…c-can't…breathe."

"Panic attack?"

She nodded, seeing swirling lights before her eyes. Her head moved against his shoulder. "Closed in. Dark. My hands."

"Kristen, slow down." Nick spoke slowly, softly. "Breathe."

"I can't. I can't."

"Yes, you can. I've seen panic attacks before. You know, men and women locked behind bars for the first time have them a lot. And lots of people in school before tests." He emitted a humorless laugh. "But I've never been responsible for getting someone through one."

"You—you're not responsible for me."

"Sure I am. Think of sunshine, fresh air." He spoke in a gentle, soothing tone. "It's warm and smells like pine trees and maybe someone's barbecue. And that was a mistake. I'm hungry now." The twisting of her middle suddenly felt more like hunger pangs than anxiety.

"You're going for a run," he continued. "You like to run, that's obvious."

She liked to run away from things that bothered her.

"We're running together along the lake. That's hard, running on sand. But—"

The van slewed around another corner and Kristen flopped against the far wall with a groan of pain.

"Are you all right?"

She hauled in a wheezing breath. "Breath knocked from my lungs. I'll have bruises. I think I'm okay now, though."

At least the panic attack had fled without becoming fully blown. Yet as her mind cleared, she thought of other things, like why the men had been at the rendezvous hours early, why the marshals hadn't been there, what these men would do to them. She and Nick had seen their faces. The men hadn't tried to conceal them.

"Nick?"

"What is it?"

"Do you think the marshals or the FBI or anyone will find us before they kill us?"

"It's entirely possible. But I don't think they plan to kill us."

"Of course they do. We saw them." She was calm now, perhaps too calm. *Resigned* might be a better word to describe her mental state.

"We'll do our best to stop them from something that drastic. It wouldn't be good for their futures."

She laughed. "Nor ours." She fell silent then. So did Nick.

Kristen fixed her concentration on ways they could get free. How to free their hands so they could untie their feet. They could run. Even if she had sore feet and Nick no shoes, they could run to safety.

The van stopped. Doors near the front opened and closed, and then footfalls crunched down the side. The back opened to twilight and a rush of cool air smelling of pine trees, damp earth and water.

"We'll untie your feet so you can walk." The burly man was still the only one of the men to speak. "Don't even try to run."

Nick met Kristen's gaze for a moment. His lips curved in a half smile. Trying to reassure her. It didn't work.

Two of the guys dragged Nick out of the van and let him stand before cutting the ropes around his ankles. If they did the same to her, she wouldn't be able to kick one of them.

Patience, she told herself. *Wait for your moment.*

At gunpoint, the men marched them into a one-room hunting shack with a kerosene lantern for light and little furniture. They bound Nick to a kitchen chair with duct tape. Kristen they ordered to the sagging sofa and secured her ankles.

"Why do you want me?" Kristen asked.

"Not for me to say. The boss'll be here by midnight." The leader of the gang made his announcement, then blew out the lantern and left the cabin. He slammed the door so hard the structure shook. From the outside, Nick caught the scrape of a hasp sliding over a ring, then the click of a padlock, leaving Kristen and Nick tied and locked in darkness to wait for midnight.

EIGHT

The van drove away. They were locked in and alone.

Kristen concentrated on breathing slowly. She must not panic now. They had three hours or less until someone came to see them. What he wanted, or what he would do to them after he told them, she could only guess. She didn't want to guess. Her imagination proved too vivid in the darkness.

"We have to get out of here before the boss comes, don't we?" Kristen spoke to dispel the images flashing across the inside of her eyelids.

"It is a good idea." Nick's voice was low, calm, soothing. "I expect there's at least one guard outside, though, so we need to be quiet about whatever we do."

"Do you think he can hear us talking?"

They were at least ten feet apart and the woods were quiet save for the sigh of wind in the leaves.

"Depends on where he's waiting."

Kristen held her breath, listening for the betraying sounds of anyone outside. At first, she heard only the pervasive silence, and then she caught the swish of fabric against the wall of the shack followed by the crunch of a footfall on gravel.

"He's in the driveway or road or whatever we came in on." She shifted on the sofa and a spring poked her leg. "Ouch."

"What's wrong?"

"Broken spring." She tried to move away from the protrusion through the sofa's worn upholstery and fell sideways against the wooden arm with a soft cry.

Nick's chair scraped against the floor. "What's wrong? Are you hurt?" He sounded anxious.

He mustn't be anxious on her part. She had dragged him into this mess, endangered his life through her own impulsiveness, her need to prove she wasn't a disappointment and useless.

No, she was worse than that—she was a menace to others. If Mom wasn't freed, this would all be for nothing.

"I just tipped over trying to move away from that spring and the arm is wood."

She couldn't sit upright with her hands bound

behind her. She needed more time at the gym doing core strengthening exercises.

If she got out of this.

"Did you get away from the spring?" Nick asked.

"No, it's still poking me."

"Hmm." With that enigmatic sound, Nick fell silent.

Footfalls moved close to the cabin again. Light flashed across the structure's only window. The guard held a flashlight, a powerful one.

In that moment of illumination, Kristen saw Nick with his head bent as though he were defeated, or maybe praying, his hair dry now but tousled, and she experienced the oddest wish to smooth down the dark waves, learn if it was as soft as it looked.

Whoa. Where had that come from? She might like Nick, but she didn't like-like him, as she and her girlfriends had said in school. He was not at all what she wanted in a man other than his kindness, his courage, his intelligence…

She moved again, and the spring dug right through her jeans to her skin. "Ouch. This thing is really sharp. I can't get free to help you—" She stopped, realization dawning on her. "If I could slide down—"

"Shh." The caution was quick and sharp from Nick.

Kristen saw the line of light around the door then and understood—the guard was right outside, within hearing distance. She must not let him know what she might be able to do.

Might was the operative word. She had to slide off the sofa so her bound hands were on the seat and near the protruding broken spring. She might be able to manage it if she went slowly. If she descended too quickly, she might fall over onto the floor and be stuck there.

But she had to do it. No way could Nick get himself free duct-taped to the chair as he was.

The guard moved on, circling the cabin, flashing his light across the window to give them those precious moments of brightness.

"Hold the arm of the sofa if you can," Nick said. "It'll slow your descent."

"If I turn sideways, I can grab it." She twisted her body to the side so she could wrap her fingers, numb from being pulled behind her, around the wooden arm of the couch. Gripping as tightly as she could, she used her feet to pull herself forward. Inch by inch she crept to the edge of the sofa. Then the sagging springs did the rest for her, dumping her onto the floorboards with a thud that shook the shack and wrenched her shoulders.

"What's going on in there?" The guard was at the door, banging and shouting.

"I fell," Kristen said.

The guard laughed and walked away.

"Did you hurt yourself?" Nick asked.

"Not much."

She had only rearranged every vertebrae and her shoulders. Tomorrow she would hurt. Tonight she had to ignore the pain.

Once certain she wasn't going to topple sideways, she released the sofa's arm and began to hunt for the spring. Moments earlier, the sharp metal piece felt the size of a butcher knife. Now it eluded her groping wrists. Each sweeping movement she made threatened to tilt her off balance, not to mention the ache in her shoulders. She gritted her teeth against moaning and worrying Nick, and kept looking…looking…

"Got it." The rope tying her wrists caught on the broken spring. Tears stinging her eyes from the pain, she began to saw her arms back and forth, back and forth, trying to fray the rope. The spring caught the tender skin on the inside of her wrists. Wetness warned her she was bleeding. No matter. Some scratches now were better than a bullet or worse later. Far better than Nick getting hurt because of her.

And the wetness helped. Along with fraying, the rope grew slippery, more pliable. In what felt like an hour, time in which the guard made three more circuits of the cabin, the tightness around her wrists eased, and with a yank, her right hand slipped free.

"It's done." If her ankles hadn't been tied, she would have danced a jig—if she knew how to dance a jig.

Now she needed to get those ankles free. Unlike her wrists, they were duct-taped, as the men had more time in the cabin to bind her and Nick. If she could find and grasp the edge of the tape, she could pull it free.

She drew her knees to her chest and tried to find where the tape started. Her fingers tingled as life flowed back to them. Her shoulders protested. With her hands free, she wanted to drag herself back to the sofa and lie down and sleep. She was so tired. She was so sore.

She was so not going to be defeated.

She kept looking, stroking the smooth silver tape again and again until—yes. She felt the seam. With what fingernails she had left, she scratched at that edge until she pulled up enough to grasp. Then she began to tug.

The ripping sound of the strong adhesive pulling apart sounded like a waterfall in the quiet.

"Can the guard hear this?" she whispered.

"Maybe. Go slower." Nick's voice, though low, held a note of excitement.

Her own enthusiasm pumped through her. Inch by inch, maintaining as much quiet as possible, she pulled the tape from her ankles layer by layer. She ripped it from her skin with a hiss of pain through her teeth, but remained motionless, breathing hard as though she'd been running, waiting for her pulse to slow, waiting to hear something besides blood pumping through her ears.

"Kristen?" Nick's voice cut through the roar in her head. "Don't leave me now."

"Leave you? Of course I wouldn't leave you." She wiggled her toes inside her sneakers.

Unlike the rope on her wrist, the tape hadn't cut off circulation. She could walk. She could get Nick free.

She hauled herself to her feet, ducking as the guard passed the window. "I need something sharp to cut you loose."

The flashlight from outside had given her a view of the single room. It didn't contain much, but shelves holding a few dishes and canned goods gave her hope maybe the cabin's owner kept rudimentary cooking implements there. Things like a knife. Even a little one would help. Even the blade of a can opener would be better than nothing.

So she didn't show herself through the window, she crawled across the floor, wincing at splinters and dirt and worse. Nothing had lived there for months, maybe even years, except for mice. She shuddered, yearning for hand sanitizer.

After she freed Nick.

She reached the row of shelves. Plastic plates and bowls, nothing to break for a sharp edge. Two ceramic mugs too thick to be useful if broken. A shoe box. She pulled off the lid and heard the rattle of plastic flatware. Spoons, forks and knives with serrated edges, but too fragile to be useful blades. Though she checked each shelf, she found nothing more useful, not even a can opener. All the canned goods had pull-off lids.

Pull-off lids with sharp edges.

She grabbed one at random and lifted the ring. But when she tugged, the pull tab broke off in her hand.

She closed her eyes, fighting the tears of frustration, struggling against the urge to throw the useless can against the wall. That action would likely bring the guard, who would notice she was free and tie her up again, maybe even to the other chair, and leave her as helpless as Nick.

She picked up another can. This time, she

took more care with lifting the ring and pulling off the lid. The sweetness of peaches rose to her nostrils and she started to reach in to pull out some of the fruit. At the last moment, she remembered her filthy hands and lifted the can to her lips, drinking the juice she would have thought far too sweet under other circumstances. At that moment, it was nectar clearing her head.

She set the can on the shelf and turned to Nick. "I have a can lid and a butter knife."

"A can lid? That's amazing thinking."

The praise warmed her. More than warmed her. She was blushing like he'd told her she was pretty.

She made herself shrug off the sensation. "It might be too flimsy to work, but it's worth a try. And there's a little bit of a serrated edge on the knife."

She crossed the room to kneel behind Nick's chair. The way his arms were bent and bound, he had to be grossly uncomfortable, yet he didn't complain. Tough guy. Hid his feelings. He was too calm, too composed. Compared to how she too easily cried or panicked or even laughed, he was an oak to her...squirrel?

There, she wanted to laugh. This was no time for that. She might go off in hysterics if she started laughing.

She began to saw at the tape with the knife, then the can lid. The edge nicked her fingers more than it cut the tape. She made only the tiniest of tears and had to stop and dash back to the sofa when the guard's light approached the window.

"How many times is that?" She posed the question without expecting an answer.

"Fifteen rounds, and he takes about five minutes per round." Nick's answer was immediate, confident.

"An hour and fifteen minutes. The boss could come any minute."

"He could." Nick was quiet for a moment, then said, "If you can't free me before the next round, I think you should leave."

"How? Out the window?"

"Maybe. Check if it opens far enough."

Kristen went to the window. "It will open far enough—if I can get the nails out."

"That will take too long and make too much noise. You'll have to go out the door."

"Even if I can manage that, where will I go?" *What will happen to you?* she didn't dare ask for fear of the answer.

"When you're free, head for water. That's either downhill or where the trees thin or both. I'll be surprised if you don't find other cabins or houses near the water."

"But how do I get out?"

While she worked at his bindings again, he told her how he thought they could get out. It was risky. It was uncertain. She couldn't think of a better idea. Trying Nick's plan on her own seemed even riskier. It put an end to the idea that she could exchange herself for her mother.

But that was unlikely once she freed Nick. Considering how the men had tried to kill him in the river, they didn't plan to let him live.

And her, too?

Either way, she had to ensure Nick's freedom.

With new impetus to free him, she wrapped a little tape from her own bindings around the edge of the can lid and sawed with more vigor. Having a better grip gave her more traction. The tape began to part little by little, but not fast enough. The guard was making his rounds again before she finished her work. In frantic frustration, she grabbed the tape with her teeth and gnawed through the last inch like… a squirrel.

She scrambled back to the sofa in time to avoid the guard's light. Once it passed, Nick bent to free his feet.

"We need a weapon." Nick stood. "I thought maybe a chair, but they're too heavy to swing effectively."

"The lantern?"

"Not strong enough."

Kristen thought, skimming her memory over what she had found in the cabin. Cans were too small and the plates too flimsy. But the shelves lifted from their brackets.

"One of the shelf boards." She started for the wall. "If we just pull it free, it will create a racket when everything falls off, and that should bring the guard to us where we can get at him."

"Let's do it, then." Nick joined her at the makeshift pantry. "You go stand behind the door. I'll free this then join you."

She crossed the room to stand behind the door. As the guard's light approached the window, Nick yanked the shelf from its brackets. Cans thudded, plates clattered and the silverware rained down with a tinkle like untuned wind chimes. Kristen cried out to accompany the tumult.

Footfalls thudded outside. "What's going on in there?" The guard pounded on the door. He wasn't foolish enough to simply barge into the cabin.

Nick joined Kristen on the hinge side of the door. Neither of them answered.

"I asked what's going on in there?" the guard shouted.

Kristen and Nick remained silent.

Muttering unpleasant comments about them, the guard removed the padlock and pushed open the door. "What the... Where are you?" He stepped beyond the edge of the door.

And Nick felled him with the shelf.

The entire shack shook on its foundation when the guard hit the floor. With no way to tie him, Kristen and Nick bolted outside, slammed the door, and fastened the padlock. When he regained consciousness, the man could work on getting the nails loose from the window frame and escape. Or wait for his boss to arrive. Either way, Kristen couldn't worry about him. They had to get moving.

They had to get moving faster than they possibly could, for as they turned from the door of the cabin, they caught the distant rumble of an engine and the flash of headlights through the trees.

"Run." Nick caught hold of Kristen's hand and headed for the far side of the cabin.

The trees grew thick there, a blend of pine and deciduous. Needles and last year's fallen leaves carpeted the ground, deadening their footfalls. Above them, the leaf-laden branches stretched in a canopy blocking the starlight and obliterating the moon.

They couldn't run. One of them would smack

into a trunk or branch and fall. But the men were close. Too close. Close enough Nick not only heard their voices, but caught a few words.

"Gone."

"Not far."

"No choice now."

No choice for what? Nick feared they meant no choice but to kill them now.

He moved near Kristen so he could murmur in her ear. "Walk right behind me."

She nodded, her ponytail tickling his face, then rested a hand on his shoulder, gripped it like a drowning woman clutching a lifeline.

He hoped her trust wasn't misplaced. Keeping away from the men in pursuit wasn't going to be easy in the dark woods when Nick had no idea where they were and only a vague idea of the direction in which they should travel.

He took his advice to Kristen—head for the water. He didn't hear a stream, so they were probably near a lake. First they must shake their pursuers.

He began to walk in a zigzag pattern, trying to move forward and not circle, yet not remain in a straight line. Twigs poked through his socks. They scratched the soles of his feet, warning him not to step hard and break them with a snap that would give away their location.

Behind them, the men chasing them weren't as

quiet. They plowed forward, breaking branches and rustling leaves. They also moved their powerful flashlights through the trees, beacons that pinpointed their locations and lit their way so they could move faster.

Their pursuers held the advantage of numbers. The three of them fanned out, limiting the path Nick could choose.

Forward. He must keep them moving forward and away from the shack where they'd been held. They curved to the right, then stepped to the left. A branch broke beneath Nick's foot before he could lift his weight. The snap sounded like a rifle. Behind them, someone shouted, "Northeast." Directing the others right toward them.

They needed a new line of escape. Nick made an abrupt shift to the right and squeezed between two saplings. Kristen flinched, her fingers pressing into his shoulder.

"Are you all right?" Nick paused to make sure she hadn't injured herself with something serious such as a twig poked into her eye.

"Just caught my hair on something."

Nick faced forward again and realized he had made an error in the direction he chose. They emerged on a man-made trail with starlight brilliant above them and one of their pursuers a mere hundred feet away.

"Duck." Nick drew Kristen down to hide beneath the drooping branches of a pine tree. Seconds later, the man's light illumined the path, the saplings and a strand of long, blond hair dangling from a broken branch.

Kristen stiffened beside Nick.

On the path, the man shouted, "Gotcha." He began to sweep his light from tree to tree, from crown to root.

In seconds, he would spot them.

Seeing no other choice, Nick waited for the man to point his light up, then lunged from beneath the pine tree and swung his leg around to sweep the man off his feet. He landed like a downed deadfall, his flashlight skittering away. Nick dropped atop the man's back, held him down and covered his mouth so he couldn't shout for his friends to help him, grabbing one wrist so he could twist the man's arm behind his back.

"Can you get his belt so we can tie his hands?" Nick asked Kristen.

Dumb question. The man was thrashing and bucking and trying to yell through Nick's hand. Of course she couldn't get the belt with its buckle under the man.

"I'll get one of his boot laces." She collapsed more than sat on the man's legs. Nick heard the thud behind him and felt the man's grunt of pain.

The other hunters seemed to be farther away for the moment.

"These are long laces." Kristen's voice was shaky, but otherwise she seemed calm enough. "I can tie his ankles."

"Start there, then." Nick wished he carried something like a handkerchief so he could stuff it into the man's mouth rather than holding his lips against his teeth so he could neither talk nor bite. At best, Nick's position was awkward, one knee between the man's shoulder blades, and one of Nick's hands beneath the man's jaw to hold his head back so the other hand could cover his mouth.

Work fast, he silently urged Kristen.

He didn't say anything, not wanting to make her anxious. She was doing great so far, a true partner in confining this man from giving away their position to the others. She had thought about the boot laces while Nick was still wondering what would work besides a belt. The laces would work better, were less likely to stretch and slip apart if she knew how to tie good knots.

"Here's the other one." Kristen dangled a shoelace at least a yard long, in front of him.

"Thanks." Nick gave her a rueful glance.

"Can you tie his hands too? My hands are kinda full."

"I'll try." She looked at the man's free hand waving around with fist clenched, trying to hit something other than the trail.

"Grab it with both hands from behind."

Kristen nodded and positioned herself beside Nick, shoulders touching in a way that made him feel they were a team, a partnership.

A couple.

No, nothing so drastic. They were fugitives from the same kidnappers and nothing more.

But they did work together well. Kristen managed to capture the man's wrist. The man stiffened his muscles, tried to break free.

A whimper of effort emerged from Kristen. "I don't think I'm strong enough."

"Okay. He might yell, but we can have him trussed up and be out of here before his friends find him."

He hoped the others weren't quite sure which trail the man had taken and couldn't locate him in an instant. Regardless, he had to risk it if they wanted to get the man tied up so he couldn't follow them.

He released the man's mouth and reached for his wrist. In seconds, he had his captive's hand behind his back and Kristen was tying the second shoelace around both wrists. Through it all, the man tried to shout, but his position kept his face down and the moldering leaves on the path muffled his voice.

"Can you keep his head down while I go through his pockets?" Nick asked.

Kristen moved to hold the man's head down without a word of question.

Nick searched the man with trained efficiency. The gun, Nick slipped into his pocket. In another of the man's pocket he found a packet of tissues. Stuffed in his mouth, they would keep him quiet for a while. They didn't have any way to secure his mouth shut. But a few moments would help them get farther away.

Other than the gun and tissues, the man's pockets yielded nothing. No wallet or form of identification, no pocketknife, not even a cell phone. Caught, the man would have to give up his identification willingly for anyone to know who he was unless he was listed in the fingerprint database.

Nick did not have access to that. Nor did he want to stick around long enough to get the man's name from him. He just wanted to try once for a little information.

"I'm going to lift you up against a tree now," Nick told his captive. "If you shout for your friends, I'll put you facedown again. Understand?"

"I think he nodded," Kristen said.

"Let him go, then."

Nick grasped the man's shoulders, preparing to lift him to sit with his back against a tree or drop him facedown in last year's leaves just as quickly if he tried to make a sound.

He remained silent, seemingly subdued other than breathing hard as though he were the one expelling the physical effort instead of Nick and Kristen.

"Let's go." Kristen's tone sounded urgent even in a whisper.

"One moment." Nick crouched in front of the man they had caught. "Why are you chasing Kristen?"

The man shrugged.

"You're not going to tell me, or you don't know?" Nick pressed.

The man shrugged again. "Why should I tell you?"

"So you can sit up until your friends find you instead of lying facedown in the dirt."

"You aren't going to get away," the man declared.

"We have so far." Nick smiled.

The man said something vulgar.

"You won't shock either of us with that kind of talk," Kristen said. "I've heard everything and am sure Deputy US Marshal Sandoval has too."

Nick pulled the tissues from the plastic sleeve and began to separate them. "I may as well gag you, then, if you're not going to talk."

"You don't have any way to secure them." The man's tone held a sneer.

"He can pull your T-shirt over your face," Kristen said. "You'll get it off eventually, but it won't be pleasant until you do."

Smart lady.

The man puffed out a long breath. "I only know the boss wants to know where his daughter is."

"His daughter?" Kristen sounded as bewildered as Nick felt.

"Who's his daughter?" Nick asked.

"Raven Kirkpatrick."

Kristen gasped.

So the name meant something to her.

"Now let me go," the man commanded.

"Sorry, pal, but we need to get out of here first." Nick shoved the balled-up tissues into the man's mouth as far back as he could.

They wouldn't hold for long without tying his jaw closed, but the moments he would take to work them from his mouth and shout should be enough time for Nick and Kristen to get away, especially since they now had a flashlight.

A flashlight they dared only use for a while. Nick hoped the others would see the light and think it belonged to the man now sitting against a tree with his hands and feet tied.

Holding the flashlight in one hand and Kristen's hand in the other, Nick started along the path then ducked into the trees so their captive wouldn't be able to say in which direction they had gone. Somewhere was a lake or river. Somewhere a path led in that direction. Land usually sloped, however slightly, in the direction of the water.

Nick sought for that drop in the terrain. He listened for sounds of pursuit. A distant shout warned him the man had gotten the tissues out of his mouth. A more distant call followed. Kristen's fingers tightened on Nick's. She stumbled and he remembered her bruised and scratched feet. His own feet suffered from a lack of shoes. If he looked, he suspected he would find the soles of his socks shredded.

The idea of cold, clear water seemed great, something refreshing and soothing in which to soak their sore feet. They needed medical care if they didn't want to suffer infections.

They weren't going to get anything but caught again if they didn't locate an escape route.

Nick kept them moving through the trees, avoiding trails though using them would have been faster. He didn't want to risk what had happened on the other path. Trails were too open, too exposed.

Going through the trees meant more brush, broken branches and sharp pine needles underfoot. It meant branches whipping into their faces and mouths full of leaves, as though the trees wished to gag them. But it also meant more places to hide, made them harder to locate, thus harder to pursue.

He stopped every few minutes to listen. At the moment, he heard no one nearby. The woods were quiet save for the normal nighttime noises of insects, a distant owl and frogs.

Frogs!

Frogs lived near water. In this part of the world, people usually lived near water as well.

"What is that sound?" Kristen asked.

"Bullfrog. You've never heard one?"

"Never." She hesitated a moment, then added, "When I went on vacations with my parents, we went to cities, to museums and the theater."

Nick couldn't imagine growing up swimming in hotel pools instead of freshwater lakes, walking concrete sidewalks instead of dirt paths. If—when—they got out of this mess, he would introduce Kristen to the joys of hiking through the woods during the day or building a sand castle on the beach.

And what was he doing thinking about a future spending time with Kristen? He must be too stressed and tired to think straight for those sorts of thoughts to enter his head. He didn't want to spend time with other women in case he fell in love with them.

He couldn't risk that again. Couldn't risk anyone's life again.

Nick kept them moving, Kristen's too cold fingers curled into his. "Frogs mean water somewhere close, and people usually build cabins on the water."

"Will anyone be there on a weeknight?"

"We can hope and pray someone is."

She sighed, then sighed again, and Nick realized she was breathing deeply, holding her fear, her panic, in check. He wanted to hold more than her hand, wrap his arms around her and reassure her all would be well. Except he didn't know if all would be well. The man behind the abductions wanted information about his daughter. Kristen probably possessed that information. Could she—would she—give it up? If she did, what were the consequences to Raven Kirkpatrick? Or Kristen herself?

He made himself focus on following the croaking of the bullfrogs. Closer. Closer. The trees grew thinner, farther apart. The scent of water increased. *Jug. Jug. Jug*, the frogs chorused.

They broke through the trees to a clearing

washed in moonlight. A half-moon reflected in a lake, brightening the sight of a tidy cottage with a deck built over the water.

An empty-looking cottage. The windows were shuttered and the deck empty of furniture. Though a broad stretch of water spread before them, the side of the lake on which Kristen and Nick stood held no other houses.

"What do we do?" Kristen's voice held a desperate note.

Nick knew how she felt. He had pinned too many hopes on someone being in the first house they found.

"We'll look for a boat."

"Steal it?"

"Borrow it."

"But won't the men hear the motor?"

"I'm thinking a canoe or rowboat." Nick led the way around the cottage. A mound covered with a tarpaulin looked promising.

"I don't know how to operate a rowboat or canoe," Kristen admitted.

"I figured as much."

If he found a canoe under that tarp, she would get a quick lesson in paddling. A rowboat would be better. He could handle the oars, though not as well as he could if he was rested and had eaten. Still, either would be transportation.

He moved the rocks holding down the tarp

and pulled the cover back. An aluminum canoe lay upside down on two sawhorses with the paddles tucked beneath.

"I'll need your help getting this into the water."

"Of course."

Together they managed to flip the canoe and carry it down the beach to the water. Nick told Kristen to hold the boat in place, then ran back to get the paddles. He set them in the boat and told Kristen to climb in.

She did so with so little speed her movement resembled a slow-motion film. The boat rocked, and she slumped down, gripping the sides.

"Just sit there and I'll go to the other end." Nick splashed into the water.

The cold lake and soft sand felt good on the parts of his feet exposed from holes torn in his socks. He dug his toes into the bottom to give himself purchase and pulled the canoe into water deep enough for it to float. Then he clambered over the edge and picked up a paddle.

"Hold it like this." He waited for Kristen to lift the other paddle and position her hands like his. "Great. Now dip it into the water at a right angle and draw straight back. Keep it straight or we'll go parallel to the shore instead of away from it."

"Where are we going?" Kristen asked.

"Across the lake. I'm hoping we'll find more cottages there and people this time."

He hoped to be away from their pursuers, to find a phone—or radio, if no cell service was available out here—and call the police.

He dipped his paddle and drew hard on the water. A glance over his shoulder warned him Kristen wasn't going to be a great deal of help. Her blade was too shallow, her strokes too short. Paddling a canoe took practice and built-up strength. She wasn't a weak lady, but neither was she used to this kind of strenuous workout. So their progress was slow. Twenty feet from shore. Fifty. Other than the splash of their oars, the lake and beach were quiet.

But from the edge of the woods Nick heard a shout followed by another.

"Oh, no," Kristen cried.

Nick turned his head to see light, then a flash followed by the report of a gun.

NINE

Kristen choked on the scream she tried to swallow. The men had caught up with them too quickly, too easily. She and Nick weren't anywhere near far enough from the shore. They weren't anywhere near enough to the other side of the lake.

"What do we do?" she cried.

No sense in being quiet. The men knew where they were.

"Paddle faster," Nick said.

He dipped his paddle deeply into the water.

Kristen tried to imitate the movement. Her shoulders felt like they were wrenching from their sockets with the effort. She thought she was strong. Paddling a canoe through a lake with men and guns behind them on the shore made her feel as weak as an infant.

To emphasize their power, those men fired their guns again. Across the water, the sound magnified, echoing around the open space.

Surely someone would hear. Surely someone would investigate.

Or maybe not in the Wisconsin woods. Maybe firing guns in the middle of the night was normal. Kristen didn't know. The closest she got to woods was walking beneath the trees in parks. No one shot guns in parks.

She glanced over her shoulder to see how much progress the canoe had made. Not much. To her, they seemed to be sitting still in the water.

The men weren't sitting still. They had climbed to the deck of the empty cottage. Two flashlights gleamed like staring eyes trying to pierce the darkness beyond the range of their beams.

Kristen and Nick were outside the flashlights' range, but the silver aluminum of the canoe glowed in the moonlight. Her hair must be glowing too. The part of her she considered her best feature, her prettiest feature, was now her downfall. First the strand on the branch had alerted the man on the trail where to look for them. Now she shined in the dark like her own beacon.

Another gun fired. Not a pistol. Pistol bounds weren't all that great. But this was a rifle. Kristen might not know about firearms usage in the woods, but she knew the firearms themselves.

Her boss had taken her to a firing range so she could understand the power of the weapons that too often harmed her clients.

They would have to paddle much faster to outrun a bullet from a rifle.

One round splashed into the lake mere inches from the canoe.

"Duck," Nick called.

"I can't paddle if I duck."

"Never mind. Just duck."

Never mind because her paddling was useless.

But Kristen didn't argue. She curled up on the bottom of the boat and clenched her teeth so they wouldn't chatter. Each breath was an effort.

A ping echoed off the seat where she'd been sitting. If she'd still been there—

A whimper like a lonely puppy's burst from her before she could stop it.

Another bullet hit the canoe without Kristen having any power to stop it. The round fell short of the seat and cut through the hull half a foot from Kristen's toes.

This time, she couldn't hold back the scream.

"Are you hit?" Nick's voice was taut.

"No, but there's water gushing in."

"Better than you being hit." Nick lifted his oar from the water. "Can you swim?"

"Of course."

"Then we're going into the water. Grab your paddle and stand. I want to tip the canoe over."

"I will if I can stand up."

She wasn't sure she could. The boat was unstable, worse with water oozing through the hole in the bottom.

Nick held out his hand. "Take my hand."

Gladly. He had broad, firm hands with long, strong fingers. He gripped her hand and hauled her to her feet. She clutched the paddle in her other hand. He gripped the other paddle in his. Together, they leaped into the lake. As the icy water closed over Kristen's head, she heard more gunfire.

The paddles drew them back to the surface with their buoyancy. Not a great deal of support, but enough to help keep them afloat so they could kick and kick and kick, heedless of the splashing or the wake of their passing. They simply wanted to get out of firing range as fast as possible.

To Kristen, the water began to feel as thick as gelatin, her legs as heavy as lead pipes. Though she knew doing so was probably foolish, she toed off her sneakers and allowed them to sink to the bottom of the lake. The absence of the soaked shoes lightened her legs, making kicking easier.

She longed for a raft she could simply lie on and float, for sunshine to warm her instead of the too-cool night breezes chilling her.

But she wouldn't mind Nick's hand to hold again.

She shouldn't think such a thing. He was all wrong for her. He had missed dinner with his sister. What if he were married and that was his child's recital he missed?

Crises happened in most jobs, incidents that compelled one to work late, but not as often as in law enforcement, not as important either, things that couldn't be put off for the next day to take time out for family.

Law enforcement and the law like her parents.

At least the denial of her moments of attraction to Nick distracted her. They had swum a hundred yards from shore. The shooting had ceased. Beams of light from the beach suggested the men walked around it, perhaps seeking another form of water transport.

Nick paused and pumped his legs to keep in place. "We need to get ashore. I don't think either of us can swim all the way across the lake."

"I'm sure I can't." Kristen could barely move her legs anymore. She could scarcely feel them. "I didn't know the water was still this cold in June."

"It was a late spring this year. It'll be cold all summer if this lake is deep."

"So which way do we go?"

Nick glanced around, though the moon had ducked behind clouds and the predawn hours were nearly light-free. "North."

"Which way is north?"

"To our left."

"How in the world do you know that?"

Nick touched her cheek, warming it, though she knew his fingers must be cold from the water. "I know how to read the sky for directions. Now let's go."

They turned. They swam. They encountered an islet, little more than a sandbar, and paused to rest. Kristen wanted to stretch out and sleep on the twenty square feet or so of sand and rocks and some scrubby bushes. But they needed to keep running from the man who wanted her to give him information about Raven Kirkpatrick. The woman's father.

The memory of the young woman made her feel as though the lake had invaded her veins, replacing her warm blood with the chilly water. She couldn't give him any information. She couldn't risk the girl's life that way.

Was any client worth dying for?

She didn't want to find out how she would answer that question, or if she and Nick would die. They needed to get away now, report Robert Kirkpatrick as the man who had engineered the abduction, a man out on bond while awaiting trial, and move Raven to another safe place, one about which Kristen knew nothing to tell.

Which was why she was sure, and guessed Nick also recognized, the men would kill them—because they knew too much. No return of her person had ever been planned. The men intended to take Kristen, extract information, then kill her.

On her feet before she realized what she was doing, Kristen raced to the far side of the islet and into the lake. "Let's go."

"Careful." Nick caught up with her.

They waded into the water until it grew deep enough for swimming. Then they struck out for the north shore of the lake a million miles away. Or maybe only a quarter mile away but seemed like a million or two. Kristen's arms and legs had ceased feeling like lead pipes and now resembled rubber bands—floppy and useless. She needed all her concentration to push through the water. Right. Left. Right.

Her foot struck bottom. She dug her toes into the oozing sand and lowered her other leg. The bottom. Shallower water. She could walk, difficult through water, but easier than swimming.

Beside her, Nick did the same. He gripped

her hand again and they trudged to shore where a tree-lined ledge met the water instead of beach. Kristen released Nick and tried to haul herself onto dry land, but her arms gave way and she splashed into the water.

"If I may?" Nick climbed onto the ledge, then held out his hands.

"Please."

He lifted her out of the water high enough she could kneel on the ground. "I hope there isn't any poison ivy around here."

"Me too." Nick kneeled before her. "I hate to tell you this, but I don't think there are any cottages or cabins around here for sure."

"Shocking." Kristen yawned. "A lake that hasn't had its shoreline developed to death with houses."

"I think it's too small for much development."

"Does that mean we can sleep somewhere without people finding us?"

Nick hesitated a moment, then said, "That might not be a bad idea. Let me see what I can come up with for shelter. Wait here."

He moved deeper into the woods. For a moment, Kristen's breath caught in her throat, the familiar beginnings of panic at being left alone. "He's coming back. He's coming back." She repeated the words to herself again and again.

They didn't help. Before she knew what she intended, she had curled into a fetal position on the ground, hugging her knees to her chest and gasping for air.

"Kristen? Kristen, you're all right." A gentle hand stroked her wet hair from her face, then rested on her cheek, lightly caressing. "You're all right. I'm here."

The touch, the voice, the words soothed her. Her breathing slowed. Her heart ceased racing as though it needed to escape her rib cage. But she started to cry.

"Shh." Nick kneeled on the ground in front of her and cradled her head against his shoulder, letting her weep out her fear and worry and guilt. He murmured gentle words of encouragement like "Let it out" and "We'll be all right."

She appreciated the former. She didn't believe the latter. She needed to cry to ease the emotions bottled inside her. The rest, however, neither of them could know for certain. She didn't know if anyone was all right. Her mother, her father, even Nick's family could be in danger. And she knew that she and Nick were far from out of the woods—literally and figuratively.

The little joke replaced the next sob with a chuckle, and the tears began to dry.

"What's funny?" Nick asked.

"I was thinking we're not out of the woods yet."

"Nice one." Nick groaned. "But we're probably fortunate for that. The woods give us plenty of places to hide."

"I hope so."

"Come. I found a place where you can get a little sleep." Nick took her hands in his and hauled her to her feet.

Kristen followed him along a narrow, twisting trail that had probably been used by more deer than humans, and showed her a woodland bower beneath the spreading branches of a pine. Those branches drooped to the ground, forming a "room" beneath.

"Your boudoir, madam." Nick lifted several of the fragrant limbs.

Kristen crawled through the gap in foliage and welcomed the soft carpet of fallen needles. "I doubt I'll sleep, but it'll be nice not to be walking or swimming. But what about you?"

"I've got my own shelter a few yards away. I'll be close enough to hear you if you have trouble, but far enough away to give you privacy."

So considerate, so thoughtful that she might need some time alone. And he hadn't freaked when she cried. The benefits of a man with sisters.

As if she needed to think about Nick Sandoval's benefits. "I'm sorry I dragged you into this."

"I think I'm the one who dove into this."

She smiled at his joke, then sobered. "Seriously. I should have listened and not gone off on my own."

"It's done, Kristen. You can't undo the past. You can only move on with the future." He laughed, though she didn't know why, and squeezed her hand. "Try to sleep."

She didn't think she could, but sheer fatigue overcame the discomfort of her battered feet and aching limbs, and she dozed off remembering how nice Nick's arms felt wrapped around her.

He'd only been comforting her. Nothing more. He was treating her like one of his sisters, probably an annoying one always causing him trouble. Still, she couldn't deny his kindness.

Or the fact that her feelings for him weren't exactly sisterly.

She smiled in her sleep and dreamed of a Fourth of July celebration with fireworks shooting brilliant stars and flowers and flags into the air.

She awoke gasping for breath with the realization the fireworks of her dream were, in wakeful reality, gunshots.

Nick lay motionless beneath a fallen log, the best shelter he had found for himself not too far from Kristen, and listened to the crackle of distant gunfire. He thought it came from the lake but had no idea what anyone would be shooting at dawn. Maybe their pursuers thought they saw him and Kristen. Shadows played tricks on tired men with quick fingers on their triggers.

The shooting could be as innocent as someone target practicing. At dawn that seemed unlikely, but people took odd notions of what they wanted.

Whatever the source, he and Kristen needed to assume the worst and get moving. They had been in one place for too long. They needed to find shelter and a form of communication.

Nick rolled from beneath the log and stood. He brushed down his clothes as best he could and headed down the narrow path to Kristen's shelter. Each step hurt his essentially bare feet. Every rock in Wisconsin seemed to dig into his heels. At least Kristen had her sneakers. Her feet didn't need any more assault than they had already suffered and he doubted he possessed the energy to carry her far without any form of nourishment for nearly sixteen hours.

Not concerned anyone would hear him above the singing of the birds, he whistled as he approached Kristen so she wouldn't be frightened. "It's me," he announced.

She poked her head through a gap in the branches. "I feel like a porcupine."

The corners of Nick's lips twitched.

She rather resembled one with pine needles poking from her hair like quills.

"Don't laugh. I'm humiliated enough." She brushed the tangled golden mass away from her face, her skin as white as fresh snow. "Was that gunfire?"

"Yep." He held out his hands. "Let me help you up."

"Is it those men after us?" Her eyes were huge and dark in the pale light.

"I don't know, but we need to get moving in case it is."

She took his hands and rose, her teeth sinking into her lower lip. He hoped she wasn't about to cry again. He didn't run from weeping females, not with two sisters, but neither did he like to see women upset enough to cry. He wanted to make the world all better for them, and right then, he couldn't make much better for Kristen.

He wouldn't think about how nice holding her felt. Neither was it the time to think about how well her head nestled against his shoulder.

"Let's go, then." She tugged on his hand and began to walk, back straight, ponytail fanning out in curls and tangles and a collection of pine needles like some elaborate hairdo for a costume.

He wanted to find a hairbrush, remove the band holding her hair up, and brush it smooth for her, feel the silkiness of each long strand as it ran through his fingers.

He needed to get them to a form of communication and safety before he lost all reason where she was concerned.

"Which direction should we take?" Kristen asked at a Y in the path.

Any direction away from the one I'm thinking with you.

"Right," he said aloud. "We want to skirt the lake but keep inland enough we can't be seen."

Especially if those men were still waiting for them along the shoreline. Around the shoreline.

He wondered if they should head in a different direction instead of seeking for occupied houses on the south side of the lake. The pursuers might be there already. They could tell anyone in the cottages a story about Kristen and Nick being fugitives from the law.

But he had no idea in which direction they could go to find people. Far enough east, they would reach Lake Michigan, but how far? They could be dozens of miles from the coast.

Nick walked along behind Kristen, ears open for sounds of people, either friend or foe. He couldn't hear much above the birds and wind in the trees. The chilly wind smelled damp. By now, the sun should have brightened the sky beyond the branches. It hadn't. The sky remained gray, sultry. Rain was coming. They needed to find shelter quickly or they would be soaked a second time. A third time for Nick. His clothes still felt clammy from the swim. Baggy in the knees and itchy. Kristen must feel as bad or worse. Her feet certainly must be hurting her. Rocks protruded between the layers of moldering leaves and pine needles. Stepping on those rocks hurt.

He glanced down to watch for stones and noticed one was smeared with red, with blood. Fresh blood.

Through her shoes.

He looked and saw she no longer wore her sneakers.

"Kristen?" He put out a hand and grasped her shoulder, halting her.

She glanced back, eyes huge and rimmed with dark circles of fatigue. "Yes?"

"You lost your shoes."

"I couldn't keep swimming in them, so I kicked them off."

"And now your feet are bleeding. Don't they hurt?"

She nodded.

"Why didn't you say something?" Nick began to think of how he could bandage her feet.

She shrugged. "What good would it do? It's not like we'd stop and change direction for an urgent care center."

"No, but I could bandage them."

"With what?"

He looked at himself. His clothes were filthy. Wrapping wounds in anything he might manage to tear from his shirt or pants could do more harm than leaving the wounds open to the air.

He sighed. "Good point." He touched her cheek. It was smooth and cool like some kind of special cloth; the smooth stuff Gina's wedding dress had been made of. Not silk. Too flimsy. Satin. That was it—delicate but strong. "I'm sorry you have to go through this."

"Why are you apologizing? I did this." She turned her back on him and resumed walking.

He followed, not knowing what to say. She was right. She had gone off on her own and gotten captured by those men, but he had followed her into the river instead of calling for assistance.

"I didn't have to jump in the river after you. I could have called for help," he said at last.

"And who knows what would have happened to me."

Only God knew what would happen to them now.

"We need to find a stream or river," Nick changed the subject with noticeable abruptness. "Running water will cleanse your feet."

"How do we do that?"

"We listen."

Running water was going to be coming from the sky if the glowering clouds were any indication. They could be in outright danger if lightning accompanied the rain.

All they could do was keep moving. Moving forward. Seeking shelter.

They walked in silence for a quarter hour, listening to the gurgle of flowing water. Then Kristen paused and glanced back to him.

"Should you have called for help instead of jumping in the river after me?"

"I did." He may as well be honest.

"Are you in trouble?"

"I was ordered to stick close to you and bring you into protective custody as soon as possible."

"My nanny." She sighed and trudged on.

He followed, trying to concentrate on picking up signals from their surroundings rather than thinking about what Callahan would say to him. Nick was supposed to bring Kristen in, not follow her through the Wisconsin woods. Callahan wouldn't care how difficult keeping her to safety was. The US marshal would have nothing nice to say. And if the judge hadn't been released, probably lots of harsh words instead. Getting Kristen back safe and sound would help.

He hoped. He prayed. He liked his job.

Sir, he imagined his argument, *I couldn't let those men take her in front of me when I had a chance to stop them. I know I didn't stop them, but here she is safe and sound.*

He glanced at her limping stride and added, *Mostly sound.*

So far, they had avoided getting riddled with bullets.

But they couldn't avoid the rain. It began as a smattering of drops seeping through the canopy of leaves overhead and progressed to a deluge pouring upon them like someone had turned on a thousand garden hoses.

They took shelter under the heaviest roof of leafy branches they found, Nick's arm around Kristen for some semblance of warmth. Kristen hugged her arms across her chest and shivered, teeth chattering.

"Is thi-this J-June or M-March?" she asked.

"March." Nick smiled.

Then, as abruptly as it began, the rain ceased, and the sun blazed down like August.

"Let's find a clearing where we can warm in the sun." Nick took Kristen's hand, still cold, and headed toward a sound he thought might be the splash of water.

It was. They broke through the trees to find a stream no more than six feet wide, but deep after the deluge.

"Sit on the bank and put your feet in the water," Nick directed her.

She dropped to the muddy edge, slid her feet in and gasped. "That's cold."

Nick sat beside her and dropped his own feet into the water. She was right. The water felt like snow runoff. But the sun warmed them. It warmed the flies and mosquitos too. They swarmed Nick and Kristen like they were a banquet ready to be consumed.

Kristen swatted them away. "This is why my mom never wanted an outdoor kind of vacation. She hates insects. If the tiniest fly gets into the house, she doesn't rest until it's squashed."

"We could do with some bug spray."

They fell silent. Nick knew what he needed to ask Kristen, something that would appease Callahan and help solve the case. But she looked so tired and defeated he didn't wish to disturb her.

He gave her time to rest and think, while he

pulled off the shreds of his socks and examined his own feet. They were bruised and scratched but hadn't sustained any serious damage. He would walk on what was left of his socks, the uppers, until he could obtain some shoes or flip-flops at the least.

He looked at Kristen's feet in the water. The remnants of her bandages still encircled her ankles. If he removed those strips of gauze, he could wrap them on her feet to protect the cuts.

"May I move those bandages to your feet?" he asked.

She glanced down. "I forgot they were even there they've been on so long." She moved back so her feet no longer dangled in the water, and pulled the wet gauze away from her skin. "These are kind of pathetic, but they will be better than nothing." She handed him the gauze strips.

They were sodden and gray, but better than walking on bare, cut soles.

He sat cross-legged on the bank and lifted one of her feet onto his knee. A long scratch ran from her arch to her heel. He traced it with his fingertip, seeking the heat signaling infection brewing beneath the surface.

She jumped and giggled. "Sorry. That tickles."

"I'll try not to touch you again."

The soles of her feet anyway. He wanted to touch her hand, her face, her lips.

Where had that idea come from? The last thing he needed to be doing was thinking of kissing Kristen Lang. It passed well beyond the bounds of propriety, of professional behavior. He wouldn't think of such a thing again.

"So who is Raven Kirkpatrick?" he asked to set his mind firmly on important matters and not dangerous fantasies. "Besides the daughter of a dangerous man."

"The daughter of a dangerous man." Kristen ripped up several blades of grass. "If I say more, I'm breaking a confidence."

"And client confidentiality?"

Kristen drew in a breath. "She's not a client anymore, so anything since isn't technically confidential."

Nick wound gauze around her foot. "How will kidnapping you help this man?" Nick asked.

"He probably wants to stop her from testifying against him."

"Do you know where she is?" He tied the ends around her big toe as though she were wearing thongs.

"I do. I also know her new name since I helped her get it."

"Is she in the witness protection program?"

Kristen shook her head. "She didn't qualify. But she's nineteen and free to go where she likes."

"But you gave her a new life anyway. And if those men catch you, they can force you, in probably unpleasant ways, to divulge this information."

"Yes."

"Why do they want it?"

"That's getting into the confidentiality realm."

"But I can presume that having her father find her wouldn't be a good idea."

"I can't tell you what conclusions to draw."

"Good enough." Nick tied off the second bandage. "This should help."

"Thank you." She drew her legs back and started to rise.

"Careful. The bank's soft here." Nick cupped his hands beneath her elbows and lifted her to the solid ground.

And when they stood on the grass, with the sun pouring over them like lemon sauce and her eyes, bluer than the sky, gazing into his, he couldn't bring himself to let her go. Too easily they could have died the night before. Too easily they could still die. But for that moment, they were alive and warm in the sweet-smelling, peaceful woods, and he wanted to celebrate that gift that might be all to fleeting.

"Will you think I'm awful if I tell you I want to kiss you?" he found himself asking.

Her eyes widened. Her lips parted. And she merely shook her head, her porcupine hairdo glinting in the sun.

He took the head shake and the parted lips as a no, she didn't object, and cupped her face in his hands. For a moment, their eyes met, and then her lids dropped and Nick touched his lips to hers.

TEN

Nothing felt so wonderful as Nick's fingertips on her face and his lips on hers. Kristen hadn't realized how much she wanted him to kiss her until he asked.

She had been stunned speechless by his question. She was left light-headed from his kiss.

And a voice shouted in her head, *No, no, no. He's law enforcement. He isn't right for you.*

He would miss dinners and birthdays and anniversary celebrations. He could get shot and leave her heartbroken and alone. She had no business kissing him.

She flattened her hands against his chest and pushed him away. "I'm sorry. I can't. I shouldn't have. We need to get out of here now."

She heard the frantic edge in her voice and felt her heart rate kick up a notch, then two. Her breath caught in her throat, keeping her from inhaling further. She opened and closed her mouth, gasping for air.

"Kristen, you're all right. Breathe. Breathe." Nick sounded like he was on the other side of a brick wall. "I've got you. Just breathe."

His hands gripped hers, an anchor in the storm of her panic, her need to run from what she couldn't face—her attraction to a most unsuitable man.

She breathed, drawing air in through her nose like she was going to sing. The oxygen reached the bottom of her lungs. For a moment, she was dizzy with the influx of air, and then the world returned to focus and her heart rate began to slow.

"I'm okay." She managed a feeble smile.

"Yes, you are definitely okay." Nick's smile was not feeble.

Oh, she liked him—too much for her own good. She liked him enough to make her panic at the idea of liking him.

"Ready to walk?" Nick asked.

Kristen slapped at a mosquito. "We'd better, though if we stay, the mosquitos just might carry us off and save our feet."

"I like how you can keep your humor in this situation. It shows strength."

"Strength? Me? I keep freaking out and you tell me I have strength."

"You have tremendous courage, and that takes strength." Nick offered her his arm. "Shall we?"

They walked like that, her hand resting in the crook of his elbow, for as long as the stream bank allowed. Then they walked single file, following the flow of the water. The day grew hot. Kristen's stomach hurt with hunger. After considering the risks of catching something nasty like giardia, they cupped their hands and drank from the stream. Kristen's feet cried out for a soft ottoman to prop them on. Her leg muscles yearned for a hot, soothing bath. Her head longed for a fluffy pillow.

By the time they began to see signs of civilization, she could barely set one foot in front of the other.

They smelled smoke first, barbecue smoke. Someone was cooking chicken over a grill. Kristen stopped, inhaled and nearly fainted with the wonder of the aroma. Her mouth watered and she moaned aloud.

"It does smell great, doesn't it?" Nick grinned at her. "Where there's barbecue smoke, there's people."

They followed their noses, turning the wrong way once and losing the scent, then picking it up again until Kristen caught the bang of a screen door and peal of laughter.

She stopped and clutched at Nick's arm. "What do we tell people when we walk in looking like—like vagabonds?"

"As much of the truth as possible. We tell them we were robbed and dropped in the woods."

"If they don't run screaming when they see us." Kristen's body tensed, but she held herself together.

She needed to be calm for the strangers, reasonable in speech and appearance—as much as someone with porcupine hair and tattered clothes could appear reasonable.

They emerged from the woods near the lake, presumably the same lake through which they had escaped. At least ten people, from small children to an elderly lady, ranged from the dock jutting over the water to the deck attached to the back of the cottage. Fragrant smoke rose from two grills set on a concrete slab below the deck, and pitchers of something cold, judging from the condensation on the outside of the colored plastic containers, rested on a long table in the middle of the yard.

At Kristen and Nick's arrival, every man, woman and child stopped talking, flipping chicken pieces or running. As one, they turned to stare at the newcomers.

Not used to so much attention, Kristen wanted

to crawl under the nearest bushes and hide until Nick got matters settled. As though sensing her urge to run and hide, Nick covered her hand where it rested on his arm, holding her in place with gentle firmness.

"We're sorry to intrude on your party," Nick said in a voice pitched to carry without shouting. "But we need help."

A middle-aged man with an expanding widow's peak turned his spatula over to a woman about his age, then strode forward. "What sort of help do you need?"

"We need a telephone," Nick said. "We were robbed."

"At gunpoint?" A boy of about ten sidled up beside the man. "We heard guns shooting last night and this morning."

"Yes, at gunpoint. I'm Deputy US Marshal Nicholas Sandoval and this is a witness I'm protecting."

"Do you have any proof?" the man asked.

Nick shook his head. "Taken. But I can give you my boss's phone number to call and verify my credentials."

"Some men were shooting at an overturned canoe in the lake," the boy offered.

"Finn, go help your mother with the chicken." The man gripped the boy's shoulder and turned him toward the grills.

"But, Dad—"

"Go."

The boy went, dragging his bare feet through the sand.

"Do you have phone service here?" Nick asked.

The man crossed his arms over his chest. "We have a landline. Cells don't pick up much off the road."

He wasn't making a move toward the house and presumably the phone. With his folded arms and wide-legged stance between Nick and Kristen and his family, his message was clear—he didn't believe or trust them.

"Please help us." The words croaked from Kristen's dry throat. "We haven't had anything to eat since yesterday, and we've just walked through the woods on bare feet because we had to get rid of our shoes when they were shooting at us and we had to dive into the lake to escape."

"David, let them come sit down. Can't you see they're about to fall over?" The woman the man had given his spatula to set a platter of chicken on the table then approached, her hand outstretched. "I'm Becky and this is my husband David being all macho and protective, especially with all that shooting we heard this morning. But anyone can see you two are no threat."

"You're still welcome to call my boss," Nick said.

"We'll do that." David lowered his arms and called to a teenage girl, "Madison, go get the cordless phone."

"The rest of you wash your hands and help bring out the salads," Becky called.

Chaos erupted as children and the other adults present charged into the house and began to return with serving dishes covered in plastic wrap. Kristen leaned on Nick, blinking to stop herself from crying over the bounty of food. If they were offered any, she must remember not to gobble. If they weren't offered any, she would just blubber like a baby.

Amid the hubbub, Madison returned with the phone and gave it to the man, probably her father, then stood beside him, giving Nick big eyes.

He's too old for you, Kristen told the girl internally.

But even bedraggled and scruffy with a day and a half's growth of whiskers, he looked rather good.

"Number?" David asked.

Nick gave it to him.

David started to punch in the numbers, then

stopped. "How do I know I'm not just calling some cohort of yours?"

"He'll call you back from an official location so your caller ID will pick it up," Nick said.

"That can be spoofed," David said.

Nick's arm tensed under Kristen's fingers. "Sir, I understand your distrust. But I don't know how else we can prove we are who we say we are, and you can see for yourselves we're in no shape to keep going."

"Just look up the number online and call that one, David." Becky squeezed her husband's hand. "We have enough data for that." She approached Kristen. "Would you like to come inside and wash a little before dinner? I might be able to find you a pair of flip-flops."

"Thank you."

Kristen wanted to hug the woman.

She allowed herself to be led into the house and to a bathroom, where she was provided with a towel, soap and hairbrush. She looked at the shower with longing, but settled for washing her hands and face. In the bedroom Becky led her to, Kristen found two more useful items. One was a hairbrush. With its stiff bristles, she managed to brush most of the tangles from her hair, then secured it in a neater ponytail.

The second item was a cell phone. For several minutes, she stared at the device in its sparkly pink case. No bars in the house, but nearly a full battery. It would work outside, maybe in the woods, definitely near the road.

Taking it would be stealing. No, borrowing. She would give it back or replace it as soon as she could. She had stolen nothing more than an extra cookie in her entire life. The guilt might burden her like a lead ball chained to her ankle.

She argued with herself back and forth until Becky appeared with a pair of sweatpants, that turned out to hang loose and fit like capris on Kristen, and rubber flipflops. By the time she finished changing her clothes, she had made up her mind.

The phone didn't show through the pocket of the over-sized pants. Having a way of contacting the outside world left her feeling oddly buoyant.

Then she walked onto the deck and saw Nick staggering back a step, the phone pressed to one ear, his fingers splayed against the side of his head. His eyes were squeezed shut, and when he gave the phone back to David, his hand shook.

Kristen had seen such looks on too many clients not to know what it meant.

Nick had received terrible news.

"Nick?"

Hand shaking, Nick returned the phone to

David and turned in time to see Kristen leap
from the deck without benefit of the steps. Her
knees buckled when she landed, but she staggered forward to maintain her balance and continued toward him at a staggering run.

"Nick." She held out her hands.

He caught them, stopping her forward momentum. "Whoa there. What's wrong?"

"That's what I want to know." She gazed at
him, her pupils dilated. "Is it my mother? Did
those men hurt her?"

"Your mother is fine."

The only part of this situation that was all
right.

"The men actually released her like they said
they would."

"Whew." She sagged. "I didn't really think
those men had any kind of honor."

"I doubt they do. It's more likely they didn't
want to be responsible for the life of a federal
judge."

Too late, Nick realized Dave stood within
earshot.

The man's eyebrows climbed toward his re-
ceding hairline. "This is Judge Lang's daughter?"

"I can neither confirm nor deny." Nick smiled
to take the sting from the response.

David nodded as though he understood, then

waved toward the table. "Becky says it's time to eat. If you want a minute to go inside and wash, go ahead."

His attitude had taken a leap in the opposite direction now that he suspected Kristen was the daughter of a federal judge and he knew Nick was who he claimed.

At least he had been. If things went well, someone who didn't know the truth of his employment status would answer the call.

He managed a smile. "I'd like that."

"Can you wait until we ask the blessing?" David asked.

"Of course." Nick started to release Kristen's hands.

She held on. "If my mom's all right, then what upset you?"

"Later. We need to eat now."

If he could force food past the constriction around his chest.

Kristen drew her brows together as though she intended to object, but the family had gathered around the table holding hands and obviously ready for someone to pray over the feast spread before them.

She had no choice but to wait. By the time they were alone again, Nick hoped he'd know how to deliver his news to her—news she wasn't going to like.

"Come sit here, young man." The elderly lady patted the empty chair between her and a teenage boy with headphones around his neck.

Kristen was directed to a seat on the other side of the table between Becky and a woman close to her age and looking so much like her they were probably sisters. Kristen didn't pull her chair in and kept her hands in her lap, obviously unused to the idea of a family holding hands for the blessing.

Nick's family had done so all his life. For weeks after Michele's death, he had refused to join in the circle, to thank God for anything. His greatest blessing was gone. Now things were nearly as bad. He was losing his way to protect the next chance God gave him to prove he could shelter others from harm.

So he was glad he could tell the grandmother he hadn't washed yet, so didn't want to contaminate anyone with trail dirt.

David said a short but heartfelt thanksgiving for the food, for family, and for being where they could help strangers in need, then the din began. Food was passed, asked for, playfully fought over. Nick slipped away to find a sink and soap inside. By the time he returned, someone had heaped his plate with a sampling of every dish, provided him with a glass of iced tea, and everyone was introducing themselves.

The other middle-aged woman was Becky's sister. The kids belonged to both of them—Becky and David with four and the sister with two—and the older lady was David's mother. She grilled Nick on his work, on how he and Kristen managed to get around the lake, on his relationship to Kristen.

"She's a witness I'm protecting," he explained.

Memory of that kiss intruded on that brief explanation, calling him a stretcher of the truth. She was his witness he was supposed to be protecting. That was right. Yet maybe she was more to him. He didn't go around kissing women for whom he felt nothing special. He just didn't know how special, how much more to him than work she had become since they met. For a year, he had told himself he didn't want a relationship with anyone, let alone a lady afraid of her own shadow half the time. Yet Kristen had courage and strength he doubted she realized she possessed before this nightmare began.

"She's a pretty girl."

Nick nodded, his mouth full of potato salad.

Kristen was indeed a pretty woman—beautiful especially with the slanting evening sunshine glowing on her face as though she were lit from within.

He feared that light would be snuffed out all too soon.

Between answering questions and eating, he considered not telling Kristen what he had learned from Callahan. His boss didn't want him to tell her anything. He wanted her to go into the marshals' protection until Kirkpatrick was caught.

Her Honor says Kristen will only worry, Callahan had said.

But she would worry anyway.

She did, however, have a right to know, Nick concluded in the end. This directly affected her. She also needed to be warned that she was going to be placed in some sort of safe house, probably an out-of-the-way motel room with a female marshal to guard her.

While he went home to lick his wounds of humiliation and failure for having been fired from the only job he had ever wanted.

At least he would have family to lend him support. They always believed in him. He didn't think Kristen enjoyed such a luxury, such a blessing, such a gift.

Across the table, she looked as though she were about to fall asleep on her plate. Her shoulders slumped. Her eyes drooped, and she had ceased to answer questions in any more than monosyllables. But when the meal ended with scoops of ice cream over brownies, Kristen rose and offered to help clean up.

Nick followed suit. "We appreciate this meal more than we can say," he said.

"We don't let anyone go away hungry," Becky said. "And speaking of going away, do you have anywhere to stay for the night?"

Kristen's gaze flashed to Nick.

"There is someone on the way to pick us up," Nick said. "They won't be here for a few more hours, though. So in the meantime, let us repay your hospitality."

"Nope. That's what we have kids for." Becky bestowed such a loving look on her offspring it was obvious she had them for far more than chores.

Rather like how his own mom looked at him and his siblings. Kristen's expression shifted from amazed to sad to the control he had first seen outside the courthouse.

Had she ever caught that warmth from her own parents? Nick feared the answer was no.

"Feel free to hang out here until your transportation comes," David said.

"Thank you." Nick looked at Kristen. "Do you want to walk down to the dock?"

She nodded, the glow draining from her face.

Leaving the children squabbling over who would perform which task and the parents refereeing, Nick hooked his arm through Kristen's and strolled toward the lake as though they didn't have a care in the world and just wanted to enjoy watching the sun set over the water. Her flip-flops slapped against the boards of the dock, and the structure trembled ever so slightly. At the end, a boat large enough to ski behind bobbed on the waves kicked up by the evening breeze.

Nick dropped onto the edge of the dock beside the boat and patted the plank next to him. "Join me?"

She sat and crossed her arms over her middle. "Now will you tell me what's wrong?"

"You didn't tell me Raven Kirkpatrick contacted you, though she shouldn't for her safety's sake."

"She swore me to secrecy. I keep secrets even though she's not a client anymore and her call wasn't therefore confidential."

"But she shouldn't have done it if she's trying to hide from her father."

"She is only nineteen and lonely and scared. She used a burner phone and she threw it away immediately."

"But Kirkpatrick knew you worked with her and had your office phone cloned so he could know who you were talking to, even if the phone didn't give away her location."

Kristen pressed her fingers to her lips. "How?"

"People go in and out of your office all day, don't they?"

"Yes, but I'm careful with my phone."

Nick shrugged. "Not careful enough, apparently."

"So Kirkpatrick couldn't find his daughter, so he decided to get to her through me." Tears flooded her eyes. "What is he even doing out of jail?"

"He could post bond and isn't considered a threat to society." Nick hated delivering the news. "And now trial has been set and the prosecutor will bring Raven back to testify." Nick felt sick delivering the news. "I've heard of dysfunctional families, but this is some of the worst."

"It's tragic." Kristen dashed her fingers across her eyes. "Raven is such a smart, honest and kind young woman. She deserves a full and happy life where she isn't looking over her shoulder forever."

"So do you, Kristen." Nick took her hand between both of his and rubbed her cold fingers. "We need to stop this guy, and we can do it now that we know who he is and what we're dealing with."

"And in the meantime I'll be locked up like I'm the criminal." She swung her legs, came close to losing a flip-flop, and tucked her knees against her chest, feet on the dock. "Maybe Raven and I can go into custody together." Her voice held a sarcastic edge.

"We just want to keep you safe."

"Which is where we started and how we ended up here—you all trying to keep me safe until you catch this criminal the system lets walk around menacing the public and worse."

"He was accused of money laundering and fraud, nothing violent."

"As if money laundering doesn't usually come from a violent crime." She snorted. "Forgive me if I don't trust your kind of safety."

She rose to her feet in one graceful motion and strode toward the deck where the adults were gathered.

Nick watched her go, knowing he should follow, and not knowing what he would say when he reached her. "By the way, I was fired from my job because I helped you," he murmured to her back.

She would feel guilty about that, and he didn't want to lay any more of a burden on her than she already carried. Nor did he want to see her leave. Yet leave she would have to do. He gazed at her perched on the deck railing, accepting a glass of tea, the sunset shimmering golden in her hair, and feared he would never see her again.

ELEVEN

"They're going to lock me up, aren't they?" Kristen sounded more resigned than angry as they sat on the front porch steps and waited for deputy US marshals to arrive and take her back to Chicago and take Nick…home.

He sighed against the burden on his heart and gave her a truthful answer. "I'm afraid it will be a dingy hotel with a female deputy marshal for company."

"For a guard, you mean."

"Something like that."

"And they won't let me see you."

"Not for a minute."

He glanced sideways to see what her reaction was. He didn't know if he should be encouraged or dismayed by her tightly closed lids and teeth sunk into her lower lip.

As if her feelings for him mattered now. As long as this situation continued, Nick wouldn't be allowed to see her after tonight.

He clasped her hand in his just as a black SUV rolled up the driveway.

"My carriage?" Kristen's fingers tightened on his.

Nick nodded, suddenly unable to speak for fear of what he would say to her, things wholly inappropriate for the moment, the circumstances, their short acquaintance.

But oh so true.

He rose, drawing her up with him. They stood tall on the steps, darkness ahead of them, lights from the porch and house behind. Pure silhouettes. Pure targets.

Targets? That was a ridiculous—

Nick caught the muzzle flash in the trees. "Kristen, get down."

His hands on her waist, he lifted her and spun her to the far side of the steps in one move. She didn't fight or scream. She dropped and rolled under the porch, then out the side.

Nick followed, counting shots, fighting spiderwebs enfolding him.

Two. Four. Six. Direction? East. Between them and the road. Beyond the government SUV. Bullets pinged off the Escalade. Two shooters. Countless rounds of ammunition. Screams inside the house.

No sound from the marshals.

Shot in the initial firing? Simply hunkered down in the SUV? They weren't firing back.

Nick didn't like that. Even hunkered down, they would try to get off a shot or two.

No time to check on them. Kristen was his responsibility. She had nearly reached the trees on the other side of the clearing. Nick sprinted after her, grasped her arm to stop her. "I need you to hide while I check on my coworkers."

"And get yourself shot?" Kristen spoke in a screaming whisper. "You're nuts to go back."

"They could be hurt."

"And they could be in on it."

Nick stared at her, though he saw no more than the blur of her face in the darkness beneath the trees. "You think two deputy US marshals are conspiring with Kirkpatrick?"

"Why not? The shooting began as soon as that SUV pulled in. If your friends didn't lead them to me on purpose, they're too careless to have their jobs."

"But Kristen—" Nick stopped, unable to find a good argument other than, "They took a vow to serve the country."

"Right. And law officers have never broken those oaths before."

"Not these two. I happen to know these two. We started in the service together."

"Can you declare that for certain?"

Nick opened his mouth to say, "Of course I can." But knew he couldn't for certain. At the least, they had been so careless they brought Kirkpatrick's men right to Kristen.

And him.

For the moment, the shooting had stopped. Not good. The men could be sneaking through the woods to find him and Kristen.

"Regardless," Nick said, "you need to hide."

"Of course I do, but you won't know where." A sob broke through Kristen's words.

Nick raised his hand to touch her cheek.

She brushed it away and plunged into a thicket of saplings and underbrush.

He stood motionless, listening to her go, listening for what might lay too close, listening for his coworkers Dillon and Belk.

He had to go back. He needed a weapon, if nothing else. He couldn't protect Kristen without one. And whether she was right or wrong about the loyalty of Dillon and Belk, she needed to be protected.

Yet if he returned to the SUV, he might be shot, captured, permanently separated from Kristen while she ran through strange woods by herself, two men and two deputy marshals in pursuit.

Nick kept to the shelter of the trees as long as he could. When the trees ended, he ran to the

SUV in a zigzag pattern, making himself a less reachable target. As he approached the vehicle, the doors opened and Dillon and Belk slid out.

"Get into the house," Belk commanded.

"You're not going after Kirkpatrick's men?" Nick stared at them as he backed toward the porch, casting his glance from his coworkers—former coworkers—to the treeline. "Won't we endanger the family by going inside?"

"Kirkpatrick's men aren't going to shoot an innocent family," Dillon said with a lack of conviction.

They had taken an innocent judge. They had run Kristen and her mother off the road regardless of the accident they could have caused.

"Give me a weapon and I'll go after them," Nick said.

Belk snorted. "Can't do that. You're on administrative leave."

What a nice euphemism for being fired.

Nick felt sick. Kristen was in those woods without support. A kind and generous family were in the house, too quiet. And somewhere nearby, men fired guns indiscriminately because—

"They wanted to separate me from Kristen." Nick spoke aloud.

Belk and Dillon's gazes snapped to him. "What?"

"The gunfire. They knew I'd go after them without Kristen." Nick applied all his willpower to stop himself from charging into the trees after Kristen.

Not without a weapon. He was nearly useless to her without a gun. He had to get Dillon away from Belk. Dillon was more flexible than their female coworker, who was determined to be a U.S. marshal one day.

"I was sent here to separate you from her," Belk said. "She needs to come with us. Now get into the house so we can go after her, or I'll have to take you into custody."

She would, too.

Nick studied her impassive, hard face for a moment, mind whirling around the notion that her orders to separate him from Kristen hadn't come from Callahan, but from Kirkpatrick's men. Yet that kind of betrayal to serve her country didn't fit into her ambitions. Still… And was Dillon on the right side or wrong?

Deciding his best course of action for the moment was to go along with Belk and Dillon, Nick inclined his head and spun to bound up the porch steps. "It's Nick," he called before pulling open the screen door.

The family had closed the storm door and locked it. At Nick's knock and repeated call, someone opened it to the extent of the security chain.

"What's going on?" Dave asked.

"Nothing that will harm you." Nick closed his eyes, hoping he spoke the truth. "They have other things to occupy themselves now."

Kristen alone.

Nick pictured her having one of her panic attacks, shaking and vulnerable to men who wanted to hurt her. Maybe to kill her.

If Dave didn't open the door in a few seconds, Nick feared he would kick it in out of pure frustration.

He kept his voice calm, light. "We need to make some plans and the SUV is too vulnerable."

"My wife and children are vulnerable," Dave said. But he released the chain and opened the door.

Nick, followed by his coworkers, stepped into the now dark and quiet living room. Murmuring voices, sounding more excited than frightened, drifted down the hall from the kitchen along with a spill of light.

"I've been ordered to stay here with you all," Nick told Dave.

That line of light from the kitchen showed the relief on his face. "I can't turn away strangers in need like you and the lady were, but I wish it wasn't so dangerous."

"Me too," Nick said.

"You and your family will be just fine." Belk spoke with so much assurance she was difficult not to believe.

Assurance because she knew what Kirkpatrick's men intended to do next?

She turned to Nick. "Do not leave here without permission."

If he was fired, he doubted he needed to take orders from her, but he hated to lie, so he merely shrugged.

"We'll find your lady," Dillon said.

"Of course we will." Belk set her mouth in grim determination.

Not if I can help it.

Out loud, Nick said, "Sure."

"Do I need to secure you here?" Belk glared at him from narrowed eyes, and she drew a set of zip ties from her pocket.

"I think that's a little extreme." Nick took a step back.

He could run through the house and get away from Belk, probably Dillon as well, but he needed to get a weapon off one of them. Somehow.

"What's going on here you aren't telling me?" Dave glanced from Belk to Nick.

"Nothing you need to worry about," Nick said. "These two will be gone momentarily." As though he planned a nice rest, he settled onto an armchair by the door. "Keep yourselves safe."

"Dad," one of the girls called from the kitchen, "can I go outside? I think I left my phone on the picnic table."

"Not now," Dave called back.

"Lock your doors behind us and stay inside." Belk spun on the heel of her boot and yanked open the door.

In silence, Dillon followed. Before he drew the storm door closed behind him, he met Nick's gaze and nodded to a bookshelf crammed with well-worn paperbacks and lined with chunks of interesting rocks. Then he, too, was gone, both of them headed in the same direction Kristen had taken not long enough ago.

"I'll get the door." Jaw hard, Dave locked the deadbolt and reached for the security chain.

Nick scarcely registered the departure. He kept hearing Dave's daughter saying her phone was outside, and seeing Dillon's nod to the bookcase.

First things first.

Heart racing, Nick circled behind him and began to examine the contents of the bookshelf. As he had hoped, as he realized he had prayed, he found a small but serviceable pistol tucked behind a hefty dictionary on the top shelf.

He was now armed, thanks to Dillon's sleight-of-hand with what must be his backup gun.

Nick tucked it into his waistband at the small of his back. "You might want to tell your family what's going on," Nick suggested.

Dave emitted a humorless laugh. "I don't know what's going on."

"It's a long story, but be assured, the marshals have Kristen's best interest at heart."

"And those people who were shooting?"

Nick sighed. "They do not have Kristen's best interest at heart. But we—the marshal service, that is, and probably local law enforcement—intend to stop them."

Unless Belk and/or Dillon were crooked.

"I'm not sure I should tell my family what's going on." Dave attempted a chuckle. "But I need to find a way to entertain them until bedtime."

"Go ahead," Nick said. "Precautions are probably unnecessary, but better safe than sorry." He returned to the chair by the door.

"Join us?" Dave asked.

"Thanks, but not now." Eyes closed, Nick leaned back as though intending to take a nap.

"Come in if you change your mind." Dave headed for the kitchen.

Before the man was halfway down the hall, Nick was on his feet, security chain off the door. Releasing the deadbolt took only a second, then he was through the doorway and racing for the trees. First, he would draw Dillon and Belk away from the direction Kristen had taken. Then he would find her or Kirkpatrick's men…or both together.

Kristen felt guilty about borrowing the cell phone, especially when it might prove useless. She knew of only one person to call. She had never asked him for help in her life, but not because she hadn't wanted to several times. She wanted a father who would come pick her up when a date wasn't behaving himself. She wanted a dad she could ask for help with math or history or just an opinion essay she was required to write. That man hadn't existed in her life. He hadn't even been around for her to tell him his wife had been kidnapped. Kristen didn't know if he would be available this time. If he wasn't, she didn't know whom she could ask for financial assistance to stay safe, to stay out of the marshal's prison of a protection.

But she had to try.

Feet throbbing, she reached the paved road. It wasn't heavily traveled, but more cars than she liked sped along the blacktop. Tucked between trees on the side of the road, she didn't know which vehicles held danger either in the form of the marshals coming for her, or Kirkpatrick's men likely still trying to track her down. She needed to keep out of sight.

That meant moving deeper in the trees and more difficult walking.

She had no choice. She stepped off the road and into the trees so she could hide. The growing darkness helped. She crouched behind a tree and pulled the phone from her pocket.

Two bars of service. Good enough—she hoped.

The phone was locked, but the virtual assistant didn't require she use a password to make a call.

She pushed the button and prepared to speak the number she had made herself memorize. "Call three, one, two, five, five, five, twenty-five, twenty-five."

"Calling," the disembodied voice responded. Then…silence.

Kristen held her breath, fearing the call wouldn't go through, fearing each car that passed held Kirkpatrick's men, who would spot her despite her cover, and pull her from the underbrush.

Her heart began to drum against her ribs. Her breath caught in her throat.

"No, no, no." She fought back the rising panic.

And the phone began to ring. One… Two…

If he didn't answer, she didn't know whom else to call. Her list of numbers had gotten soaked in the lake and she hadn't memorized any others.

Three… Four…

Nausea clawed at her middle.

Five—

"Stephen Lang."

Relief sent the breath whooshing from her lungs and she couldn't speak.

"Hello?" Cell towers and satellite relays couldn't mask impatience in the voice on the phone.

Kristen swallowed and tried again. "Daddy, this is Kristen. I need your help."

"Kristen, where are you?" Impatience gone, her father now sounded frantic.

"I'm not exactly sure. Where are you?"

"I'm in the Geneva airport waiting for a flight home."

"I've been trying to reach you for days."

"I know. I was on retreat. Deliberately in-communicado. Your mom and I— Never mind. Are you safe?"

"For now. But I need money to stay safe."

"I thought the Marshals Service—"

"Never mind them. They want to lock me

up like I'm the criminal. Can you wire me money?" she asked.

"I can, but are you sure? You're safer—"

"Please." She felt only a twinge of guilt when she added, "I haven't asked you for anything since I was fifteen."

The year her mother became a judge and her world exploded.

Maybe he would remember that birthday dinner he hadn't bothered to come home to.

He was so quiet she feared the call had dropped. Then his breath sighed across the speaker like a gust of wind. "How can I send it to you?"

She gave him as much information as she'd been able to glean from Becky about the local town. Her father could do the rest, or have his assistant do the rest.

"All right, sweetheart, but I hope you decide to go with the marshals instead."

She ignored what he said except for the "sweetheart." He had never called her anything but Kristen all her life.

She cradled the phone against her ear. "Thanks, Daddy. I've got to go." She disconnected the call.

Calmer than she'd felt for days, she rose and tucked the phone into the crook of a branch. Now she needed shelter. If she remained along the road, someone would find her. Yet if she ducked into the woods, she might get lost, go around and around in circles until she ended up where she started. Without a light, she might also fall and break something, or encounter a wild animal. Weren't bears in these woods? Bobcats? Did Wisconsin have poisonous snakes?

She wrapped one arm around a tree, gasping for breath as though she had just run a mile uphill.

"Not now. Not now. Not now," she said aloud, though not too aloud. Just enough to relax, remind herself she needed to keep calm, remain in control.

Her breathing steadied. Her heart slowed. And she began to walk through the trees, attempting to remain within hearing distance of the road and out of sight of drivers. Those trees made the woods darker than the night had been in the clearing. Branches interlocked overhead. Heavy with leaves in June, little moonlight reached the ground. Brush tangled underfoot— fallen limbs, tiny trees struggling to gain hold beside their larger parents, enough old leaves to keep someone raking steadily for a month.

She remembered raking as a child. She had grabbed the landscaper's rake and taken the task on herself. Her shoes had grown wet and muddy. Her hair had caught on low limbs and been pulled from her pigtails, and her muscles ached, but she had loved every minute of the fresh autumn air, the spicy scent of the leaves, the pretty colors. When she created a huge pile of leaves, she had run and jumped in them laughing and laughing until the housekeeper noticed and marched Kristen inside to face the music.

That music had come from her mother. Kristen was supposed to be practicing the piano, not playing outside. She was supposed to stay neat and clean for a birthday party later that afternoon, not go rolling around in the mud like a farm animal.

Her outdoor excursions were all regulated after that—scheduled strolls through nature preserves, guided tours through conservatories, catered picnics in suburban parks. Even after she attended college—locally—and moved into the condo her parents bought for her, she hadn't taken advantage of the freedom of adulthood and independence. Regulated outings had been too engrained into her system for her to think about simply wandering through the woods.

"I could have picked a better time and place to start." She laughed at herself.

Though that was a mere whispered chuckle, it sounded like a shout.

She stopped, afraid she had gotten too far from the road and was meandering into the type of area one saw on the evening news, the sort where they found the person a week later half-dead from starvation, thirst and exposure. If she had gotten off course, she didn't know which way to turn to get back on it again.

The stillness was profound. She shivered, though the temperature couldn't be much lower than the midsixties. No matter how long she stood there, she heard nothing but, eventually, faint rustling in the underbrush and the distant hoot of an owl.

She had moved too far away from the road.

"Do. Not. Panic."

Too late. Her breathing rasped in her throat. Her heart beat out of control. She dropped to the ground and hugged her knees to her chest, gasping, shaking, hugging her legs against herself to protect her body. She sobbed in frustration, in anger with herself. Someone was going to find her making all this racket. Someone was going to be able to walk right up to her and carry her off to a safe house for her own good for who knew how long, or to another hideout in another forest to compel her to divulge the whereabouts of a young lady who was trying to live as normal a life as possible and get an education.

She didn't know how long she huddled on the ground. Time ceased when these attacks crashed upon her. Eventually the shaking stopped, her breathing slowed, her heart resumed its normal rhythm. She was able to pull herself upright with the help of a tree. She leaned against it, waiting for the dizziness to end. Once her vision cleared and her ears returned to hearing the nearly nonexistent noises of the woods instead of blood roaring through her ears, she started walking, veering right. Certain the road lay in that direction if any.

Or as certain as she could be.

To herself, she sounded like an elephant tramping through the trees. No matter how lightly she trod, twigs snapped and crackled beneath her feet. Leaves rustled like a high wind passed through them, though she didn't feel so much as a breath of a breeze. Afraid she was announcing her presence to anyone who came within a quarter mile of her position, she stopped every few minutes to listen for the betraying snaps and swishes of another person in the woods. Each time, she sighed with relief at hearing nothing. The next time she paused, she heard an engine, something powerful like a semi. That meant the highway must be nearby. She had gone in the right direction.

That gave her courage to continue. If the

highway was to the east of David and Becky's cottage and Kristen kept that highway on her right, she was going north. The town she wanted lay north. So, she hoped, did some sort of place she could stop for the night. Her strength was flagging. Her eyes burned with fatigue. Her feet caused her pain with each step. She had to force her aching legs to take one more stride, one more—

Her next step met empty air. She tried to throw herself backward and only succeeded in throwing herself off balance. Her other foot slipped in mud and she fell, sliding, then rolling down an embankment and into a body of water.

Water no more than two feet deep, a lazy creek or culvert flowing so slowly she hadn't heard it gurgle, so overhung with trees she hadn't seen a gleam of moonlight on the water.

She landed with a gasp and a cry, then sat in the water stunned, mortified, and listening to heavy footfalls rushing toward her.

Nick heard the crash, splash and cry and knew he had found Kristen. Risking the flashlight being seen from the road, he flicked the switch and charged toward the source of the sounds. The instant he spotted her already rising from the water, he switched off the light.

"Kristen, it's me," he said in a low tone. "Don't run."

"Don't run when Kirkpatrick's men are after me?" Her voice held an edge sharp enough to chop down a tree. "And your agency that wants to lock me up like I'm the criminal?"

Nick sighed, unable to deny the truth of her claim. "I'm no longer a deputy US marshal."

"Just for helping me. That seems unfair."

"Me helping you was just the excuse Callahan has been looking for to get rid of me."

"Sure it is." She started up the bank.

Nick held out his hands. "Let me help you up."

"Won't you get into more trouble?" Despite her words, she took his hands and allowed him to help her climb the steep, muddy side of the creek.

"I might. But if I can prove Kirkpatrick is behind the kidnapping of your mother and the attacks on you, I will get back into enough people's good graces that Callahan's opinion of me won't matter." He still held her hands. Her fingers were freezing and he drew them together between both of his palms and rubbed them to warm her.

She didn't object. "How do you propose you do that?"

"I figure if I follow you around, Kirkpatrick will catch up with you and I can capture him."

"That's—that's—you aren't serious." The words emerged on a quiver as though she were about to laugh or have hysterics.

"Not entirely." He released her hand and touched her cheek. "Completely seriously. Kristen, did you think I was going to leave you to be on your own?"

"I didn't know. You seemed suspicious of your own agency and you stayed behind."

"I stayed behind so I could get a weapon to help defend you or free you, if necessary."

"Did you?"

"Thanks to Dillon."

"So he's a good guy?" She sounded hopeful.

"I think so. Jennifer Belk I'm not entirely sure of. Yet. But they don't matter if we steer clear of them."

"I've managed so far." She drew in an audible breath as though about to make a confession. "I also got ahold of my father. He's wiring me money to the nearest bank. I'll pick it up in the morning and…go to Canada or Europe or something until Kirkpatrick is caught."

Nick startled as though she had shoved a pointed stick into his middle. "Isn't that ruining your life as much as having the Marshals Service put you in custody?"

"Not at all the same. I'll be able to go off on my own, to eat when and what I like, to…well, feel in charge of my life for once." She snorted. "I doubt you can understand that. You've probably had charge of your life since you were born."

Nick started to agree, and then he thought about Monday night dinners with one sister, Wednesday night meals with one brother and family meals on Fridays. Every week the same, de rigueur. Command performances. He thought about how Callahan assigned him to the worst, the most boring duties and criticized every move he made. Even joining the marshals hadn't been one hundred percent his choice. Someone from every generation of his family served in law enforcement of some sort. None of his older siblings had gone in that direction, so the career path was chosen for him.

"Not entirely," he said at last. Then he smiled. "In fact, I'd say right now you're dictating what I do."

She started to turn away. "I didn't make you come after me."

"I said I would. I never had any intention of letting you remain on your own if I could help it, not with Kirkpatrick after you." And not wanting to be away from her for more than an hour, his heart reminded him. "I haven't seen nor heard a peep out of anyone except you, so I'm thinking the marshals gave up and are waiting for daylight or more men to look for you. Maybe Kirkpatrick's men did the same."

"May we rest, too?"

"When we find shelter."

"How do we do that?"

"By trial and error."

"With me as the trial?"

Nick laughed and wished he could kiss her again. He shouldn't have done so earlier that day, a lifetime ago, or so it felt like. But she was funny and kind and so very pretty she drew him like a soaring seagull to breadcrumbs. No, breadcrumbs were too plain. More like a cat to something shiny.

They had to get moving before he did something stupid.

"Any way you look at things," he said, "we've been standing here too long."

"Especially after all the racket I made when I fell." She squeezed his hand.

"Which is just one reason why I think the others have given up for the night. You were too easy to find."

"Only when I fell."

"True. But no one's come along since I got here."

"Then let's get out of here."

They got going, Nick in the lead, guiding them along the creek away from the road in the hope of finding a deer or man-made trail leading to the water. They risked others finding the same trail, but they would hear anyone coming early enough to hide. They could also move more quickly on smoother land and were more likely to find someplace to shelter like the porch of a cabin empty for the week.

Nick found the trail. Along the bank of the creek, the brush and grass lay trampled from small herds of deer drinking there. Compared to the darkness between the trees, the clearing seemed spotlighted, bright enough for them to notice the narrow trail that led back toward Becky and David's cottage, or continued north on the other side of the creek.

"Can you cross it?" Nick asked.

"I've already gone swimming in it. Wading is nothing."

Nick made his way down the bank, not as steep here, then helped Kristen. His borrowed sneakers worked much better than her second-hand flip-flops. The water reached their knees and was ice-cold. One of Kristen's flip-flops stuck in the muddy bottom and they spent five minutes fishing it out. It was a necessary delay. They couldn't continue without her footgear, however flimsy.

Once on the other side of the creek, they continued at a faster pace. Several times, Nick paused to ensure Kristen was doing all right. Other than breathing hard, she said she was. He didn't believe her. His feet hurt. Hers had to be in agony. Nonetheless, she kept up with him.

Sometimes he paused to listen for signs of other people in the woods. Aside from the distant rumble of an engine now and then reminding him they weren't far from the highway, neither of them caught the telltale noises people made—crackling leaves, snapping twigs, a cough, a sneeze. Nothing. Just those cars on the highway.

They walked without speaking until the wind kicked up and the sky grew darker, stars and moon blotted out. This wasn't predawn. This was a storm coming. They not only needed to get out of the bad weather, mud would show the direction of their footprints. Yet they had come across nowhere Nick considered shelter, not even the sort of large pine tree under which they could crouch for protection, especially not protection if thunder accompanied the storm.

"Start praying we find someplace soon," Nick said. "This feels like it could be a rough one."

As though emphasizing his impression, lightning flashed above the trees. Nick started to count. "One thousand and one, one thousand and two..." He wasn't quite to five when the thunder rolled across the sky.

"What was that about?" Kristen asked.

Her hand trembled in Nick's.

He squeezed her fingers to reassure her. "The storm is about a mile away. Sound travels at about eleven hundred feet per second, so five seconds are about one mile if you count between seeing lightning and hearing thunder. Did you never learn that?"

"No."

"Now you know. Let's go. We need to get out of these trees before this gets any closer."

They were nearly running when they stumbled into the clearing. One moment trees surrounded them, the next they stood in the open with lightning illuminating the scene before them like strobes—revealing the tiniest house or cabin Nick had ever seen.

It wasn't much more than a toolshed, yet appeared like a perfect house, a child's playhouse.

"It's a tiny house," Kristen said.

"You're telling me it's tiny."

"No, I mean it's a tiny house like the tiny house movement."

"You mean people really build those?"

"They really do. Look. It's adorable."

"It's...ridiculous."

But he loved her enthusiasm for the miniature structure. He also loved the fact that, tiny house in the middle of nowhere or not, it had a porch. Not a large one, but not quite as tiny in proportion to the house as one might expect, and it sported a roof.

"I don't think anyone is there," Kristen murmured. "It's dark."

"It would be. It's the middle of the night. But let's see if we wake anyone up by going onto the porch."

The first drops of rain began to fall as they climbed the two shallow steps to the concrete slab that acted as a porch base. A wooden railing ran around it and a swing hung from the ceiling. The concrete made their footfalls quieter than wood would have. They sat on the swing. It creaked. Nick pushed them back and forth a few times, allowing the creaking to continue, and listened for signs of life inside the house.

If anyone was there, they slept too heavily for the swing to wake them.

"Dare we talk?" Kristen asked.

"I think this house may be empty, but I doubt anyone will begrudge us taking shelter on their porch."

"What if Kirkpatrick's men track us here? Or

whoever lives here calls the sheriff and alerts the marshals? You'll be in serious trouble."

"I'm already in serious trouble. A little more won't hurt."

Much.

Despite asking if they could talk, Kristen sat in silence for several minutes. They watched the storm approach—the light show flashing over the trees, the concert of thunder and gushing rain. Somehow, they still held hands, and Nick felt closer to her than he had anyone in too long a time.

Then Kristen turned to him and asked, "Why does Callahan dislike you so much?"

Nick cringed, though he knew the question was inevitable.

"You don't have to answer if it's none of my business," Kristen hastened to add.

"Everyone else knows. So you may as well." Nick sighed and leaned against the back of the swing. "I was engaged to his daughter."

Kristen startled. "You were?"

"I was. We dated for two years and got engaged on Valentine's Day of last year."

He waited for her to ask what had happened or say something about Valentine's Day being romantic or cliché. She said nothing. Surprised, he looked at her before he remembered she was a trained listener.

And he needed to talk to someone who hadn't known Michele or him or both forever.

"Michele was pretty and fun-loving and smart, but she'd taken a while to figure out what she wanted to be when she grew up." Nick pictured the petite brunette who had been the love of his life for two years, and he could barely remember her face. "Her father spoiled her and never made her do anything she didn't want. But when we met at a party at her parents' house, she started to change. She decided she needed to get her act together and do something with her life. She just didn't know how. She was…needy. Someone always took care of anything hard in her life." Nick paused.

Kristen nodded in silent understanding.

"I kind of fell into the same pattern of running to her rescue—when her car wouldn't start because she didn't want to pump gas in the cold and had run out, or when she didn't want to eat lunch alone on campus." He scrubbed his hands over his face. "I guess I was starting a bad precedent for our future, but she was so grateful, and I am the baby in my family, so no one has ever needed me." He stared at the lightning flashing like cameras. "She needed me too much."

Kristen drew the back of his hand to her cheek and waited for him to continue.

when he didn't speak, "We all make choices. Michele could have taken a taxi."

"And I didn't have to take someone else's shift."

"Is either decision God's fault?" Kristen licked her dry lips. "I blamed God when I had to go into hiding for a month when I was fifteen, right after my mother took the bench. It was horrible. I've had panic attacks ever since. But the only people to blame are the men who perpetrated the crime. I've had to learn that in my work."

"Thank you." Nick's breathing grew easier, his mind clearer. "We should rest."

He thought he might be able to rest with some peace.

At the far end of the porch, a handful of beach chairs rested against the rail. Nick pulled one out of the stack and set it up. "Why don't you stretch out on the swing and get some rest if you can. I'll sit here to give you some privacy."

"But you'll be uncomfortable."

"I'll be just fine." He propped his feet on the railing and leaned back in the canvas chair.

The swing creaked. Kristen would have to curl up a bit to fit on the seat, but she might be able to rest.

He glanced toward the swing, where Kristen

lay still and quiet, her breathing even, and restlessness took over his body once more. He rose and began to walk around the tiny house. In the back, he found a driveway cutting through the trees. That would take them to the highway. What they would do once there he wasn't sure. Kristen's idea of collecting money from her father and heading for Canada was not a good one. He respected her reasons for the action, but he knew the action wouldn't keep her safe from a man like Kirkpatrick.

They needed to stop him.

Nick inhaled the freshness of the forest and earth washed clean from the rain and came up with one idea to which Kristen might agree.

He returned to find her on the porch steps, her arms crossed over her middle.

"I thought you left me here," she said.

"Reconnoitering. Did you sleep?"

"I think so, for a few minutes anyway. You?"

"No." He held up his hand in the "stop" gesture. "It's all right. I think we should go to my family's lake house. It's not that far from here with a little transportation."

"Won't someone look for us there?"

"Probably. But it's my territory. I know every nook and cranny of those woods, where to hide and how to protect you there."

"Or just bring an end to this. I have to bring an end to this."

"We'll figure out something."

"I think I already have."

Nick tried not to groan. She might work with people who were victims of horrible crimes, yet sometimes she seemed so naïve. Sheltered. Endearing and, in this situation, dangerous.

"You can tell me all about your plan on the way to town." He tried not to sound patronizing.

"Oh, town. Restaurants." She rubbed her stomach. "I'm starving. As soon as I have money, I'm buying breakfast."

"You know you're a sitting duck in town?" Nick said.

"I do." She descended the steps and approached him, her head high, her ponytail a tangled flag behind her. "I was thinking while I was lying here. I can't spend weeks, maybe even months or years, running. I don't need much, and coffee and a hot shower every morning make even the hardest days bearable. To sleep outside and wake to no water is just unthinkable."

"So you'll go into a safehouse?"

"No, I'm going to see about ending this cat-and-mouse chase."

"Kristen…"

"And the only way to catch Kirkpatrick is to draw him out. And the best way to draw him out is to be bait."

TWELVE

Kristen knew what Nick would say before his protest rang through the clearing. "No way. I won't let you."

"You can't stop me."

"I can with one phone call."

Of course he could. He might be on administrative leave from his job, but he would win brownie points if he turned her in. He would win more if he turned in Kirkpatrick, but that was another matter.

"I want you to make that phone call." Kristen spoke with confidence. She had never felt so sure of herself in her life. "I want you to call the marshals who also want to find me, but not until I do a few things myself."

"Such as?" Nick stepped in front of her, arms crossed over his impressive chest.

"Phone calls."

"To?"

She shrugged. "The media."

Nick's boss.

"You can't put yourself in danger," Nick protested further.

"I'm already in danger. What's a little more matter?"

"It all matters."

"How far is it to town?"

"A mile." Nick looked bemused, or maybe just fatigued. "And we have hours until the bank opens. We better take our time. Keeping a low profile in town isn't going to be easy."

"You're the expert."

Nick huffed out a breath. "Not expert enough to know how to talk you out of doing something really dangerous and therefore stupid. But I have a couple of hours left to try."

Kristen tucked her hand into the crook of his elbow and let him lead her down the driveway of the tiny house. The only creatures that seemed to be awake were the birds. They flitted back and forth, calling to one another and gathering their breakfasts. Kristen longed for hers. She couldn't remember the last time she woke and enjoyed a cup of hot coffee with too much cream in it, along with a bagel or muffin, something to get her going. Bacon and pancakes came later in the morning for her. Lots of syrup and fresh fruit.

She nearly groaned aloud.

"What's up?" Nick asked.

"Nothing new. Why do you ask?"

"You were just clutching my arm like you need it to stand upright."

"Sorry." She started to draw her hand away.

"Don't." He covered it with his, holding it in place against the muscles of his forearm. "I was afraid you were hurting, or hoping maybe you changed your mind."

"My feet hurt and my legs ache, but mostly my stomach is thinking about things like bacon and pancakes."

"Sorry I asked." He did groan, and they laughed.

Through all they had endured, not knowing what was going to happen in the next two hours, or the next two minutes for that matter, they could still find something to laugh about together.

He was a good man to go through the storm with. *If only he weren't in law enforcement*, she reminded herself. Yet, for some reason, the admonition not to care about a man who might have to put his career in front of her at times, who admitted he had done so for his deceased fiancée, held far less conviction than it had. The quality of the man and the strength of the bond came before any job or dinner.

But they didn't have a bond. He still grieved

Michele, even if the guilt over her death was lessening. Any moment, they could be ripped apart and pulled in different directions. Caring was dangerous.

Not as dangerous as making herself a target for Kirkpatrick. Yet she was already a target for him. She may as well do it on her terms when she had a chance to end the matter once and for all, a chance to ensure the safety of his daughter and herself and those Kristen cared about.

Like her parents, friends, Nick. She had endangered her mother. She must not endanger Nick more than she already had.

Beside her, apparently lost in his own thoughts, Nick halted. Kristen followed his gaze to where the road they traversed led onto the highway. They couldn't reach town any other way but to walk along the main road. Anyone who knew to look for them might be driving along that road. Kirkpatrick could cruise past, or one of his men could spot them.

"We have to risk it to get your money," Nick said.

"Then let's not dawdle."

Nick laughed. "Did you just use the word *dawdle*?"

"What's wrong with it? It means to delay, which is what we're doing."

"I know, but I haven't heard anyone use that

word since my grandmother passed away. She liked *dawdle* and *dillydally*."

"Not *shilly-shally*?"

And they were laughing again.

"I think we're getting hysterical with fatigue and hunger," Nick said, rubbing his wrist across his eyes, then down his cheek. "I haven't shaved in days, either. I must look like a caveman."

"I feel like something the cat dragged in and rejected." She tugged at her once again hopelessly tangled ponytail. "They may not even let me in the bank to get my money."

"How will you get it without an ID?"

"Secret questions. My father will have instructed them to ask me specific questions to which only I am likely to know the answer, such as the color of the car he bought me when I turned seventeen and got my license."

"Which was?"

"Lake blue."

"Like your eyes." His tone held such tenderness Kristen forgot to breathe until she stumbled over her flip-flops and gasped when her sore heel came down hard on a rock.

Nick stopped.

So did a vehicle on the other side of the highway, a dark SUV. Kristen forgot about her foot and glanced toward the monstrous vehicle. "That looks like the one that drove me off the road."

"Get behind me." Nick turned so he was between Kristen and the SUV.

The SUV didn't move. Kristen and Nick didn't move. No other vehicles cruised along the highway.

"What's stopping them?" Kristen felt a bubble rising in her throat like she might scream.

"I think it's just one man. Hard to tell. The windows are tinted darker than the legal limit."

"Or someone could be below the window line."

"Either way, they're probably trying to assess whether or not I'm armed."

"You are, aren't you?"

"I am, thanks to Dillon."

She shuddered. "Then let's get going and see what they do. If I stand here any longer, I'm going to start screaming like I'm having a temper tantrum."

"That sounds charming." Nick resumed walking, watching the SUV start rolling forward, creeping along to match their pace.

"This is making my skin crawl," Kristen admitted.

"I don't exactly feel good about it either. Hold on."

At the rumble of a semi engine approaching from the north, Nick edged Kristen off the berm and into the trees. The monstrous tractor-trailer seemed to barrel toward them, then plowed past, its giant tires kicking up stones and shedding exhaust like a toxic cloud. By the time it muscled its way past them, the SUV had disappeared up the road.

Kristen didn't know if she was relieved or disappointed. She wasn't ready for a showdown, not having a plan fully in place yet. On the other hand, she yearned for the whole thing to be done with sooner than later.

Signs of civilization came into view, a gas station first, a restaurant, a church. Sidewalks appeared in front of houses. Then what must pass as the downtown area opened up with restaurants, stores carrying kitschy tourist stuff and serious camping gear, and the bank. The all-important bank.

"I think," Nick said, "we should look for another church near the downtown. Churches are good places to retreat and reconnoiter."

"And pray," Kristen murmured.

"That too."

A spire rose above the commercial properties, white against the blue sky. Kristen headed for it, but Nick paused at a newspaper box on the sidewalk, his face white.

"What?" Kristen turned to read the headline

visible through the window and felt the world spinning out of control, the sidewalk coming up to meet her.

"Federal Judge Still in Hands of Kidnappers"

"Daughter Still Presumed Involved"

Suppressing the rage bubbling inside him, Nick lifted Kristen to a sitting position. Her eyes opened and she dropped her head to her drawn-up knees.

"Someone is lying to us. Is my mother all right, or is she still kidnapped?" She moaned.

"I know." Nick spoke through gritted teeth. "I thought it strange Kirkpatrick would let his men turn her over that easily. She's too good a pawn. But they probably thought you'd be more likely to come in if you thought your mom was safe and wanted you to."

"My dad didn't even know. He—" She stopped and glared up at Nick, though he understood the anger wasn't directed at him. "He didn't say anything about her. He just said he was on his way home." Tears flooded her eyes. "Everyone is still trying to protect me. I wish—"

Beside Nick, a door opened. "Is she all right?" asked a woman of about fifty, with her blond hair pulled back in a ponytail.

"She had a shock," Nick said.

"I'll be all right." Kristen kept her head down.

It was a good precaution, though probably unnecessary. The only picture the paper had of her was attending some charity garden party with her mother. They looked like sisters in their complementary summer dresses and broad-brimmed hats shading their faces.

The woman's dark eyes narrowed. "You two don't look all right. Were you in an accident?"

"We were robbed." Nick felt he spoke the truth.

"That's terrible. Do you need me to call the sheriff for you?" The woman glanced inside the store, which Nick now realized was actually a restaurant not yet open.

"The law already knows." Nick spoke the truth again, strictly speaking.

"Then why don't you come in and have some breakfast?" The woman opened the door wider. "You look like you could use a good meal."

"We could," Nick said, "but we don't have any money until the bank opens."

The woman waved off that concern. "Never mind. If I can't provide a couple of free meals to folks who need it now and then, I shouldn't be in business anymore. I'm Susan, by the way." She moved aside so they could enter.

Nick helped Kristen to her feet and followed

her and Susan into the restaurant. "This is kind of you, but you're not open yet."

"I open at eight o'clock and it's seven now. My cook will be here in half an hour, but I'm capable of cooking bacon and eggs, or pancakes if you like."

In the next half hour, she proved just that. She provided them with fresh, hot coffee and orange juice, then proceeded to present them with a feast of bacon, eggs and pancakes perfectly turned out and savory. They ate until they were full, speaking little, feeling safe tucked into a back booth where no one could see them through the windows.

"Just stay here as long as you need to," Susan said as she refilled their coffee cups. "We're not that busy on weekdays."

They sat sipping the rich brew and made plans, while the restaurant opened and began to fill with hungry patrons. Knowing he couldn't talk Kristen out of her decision, especially now she knew the Marshals Service had lied to her about her mother, Nick decided to join her.

"You know this won't guarantee they free your mother," he pointed out.

"I know nothing is guaranteed. My mother called the marshals as soon as she knew we were in trouble, and that didn't guarantee we were rescued. You said the plan for getting her back when they claimed they would exchange her for me wasn't guaranteed." She reached across the table and took his hand. "We need to have faith we will be taken care of and take what action we can."

He gazed into her beautiful eyes. "I just don't think I could bear losing another lady in my life."

That was as much as he was willing to say at that moment, a half confession that he considered her in his life and wanted her to remain. He didn't like to think of the bleakness of waking to a day knowing she wouldn't be a part of it.

"Then let's get this over with." He pushed back his coffee cup, breakfast a hard lump in his middle, and rose.

Kristen slid out of her side of the booth and waved to Susan filling coffee carafes on the other side of the dining room. Nick gave her a nod of acknowledgment of her kindness and generosity toward them. The meal had cleared his head more than he thought possible without sleep.

Scanning the street for anyone who looked as though he didn't belong in a tourist town, Nick slipped his fingers through Kristen's and walked with her to the bank. The time was one minute after nine o'clock and someone was raising the iron gate that covered window and doors at night. In seconds, they would be inside and Kristen would obtain money her father had wired to her. After that, Nick would have a difficult time stopping her from her dangerous plans to lure Kirkpatrick to her.

Dangerous because he didn't know how he could help her. His training involved teamwork, strategy, weapons. Their only strategy was Kristen's. They had become a team these past few days, yet she didn't want to work with him unless he went along with her.

A bank employee must have seen them lingering outside, for she approached the door and asked them if they had business. When Kristen said she did, the woman gave her a speculative glance from head to toe, but she opened the door wider and motioned her inside.

Nick waited in the lobby between the two sets of doors, watching, always watching—the sidewalk, the street, the traffic from business to business. He spotted a store across the street that sold Tracfones, solving one of their problems—their need for a phone. Cruising too fast up the sleepy little town's street barreled a dark SUV, the same one that had paced them on the highway. Other drivers honked at the oversize vehicle and a mother snatched her bicycling child away from the road seconds before the right bumper would have caught the boy's back wheel. She shouted at the men in the SUV, but they ignored her, speeding on with no regard for bicyclists or children.

Bicyclists. If he and Kristen could obtain bikes, they could get away faster than on foot. Renting a car was out of the question since neither had ID, let alone driver's licenses. Renting bikes might be just as bad. Maybe Kristen would be willing to buy them if he paid her back. If she could ride a bike. Given how little outdoor activity she had enjoyed in her life, Nick wouldn't be surprised if she didn't know how to ride a bike.

Kristen emerged from the bank with her hand pressed to a noticeably fatter left front pocket and a tentative smile on her lips. "All done." She didn't meet his eyes. "Ready to go?"

"Depends on our destination," Nick said.

"The cell phone store."

"So you noticed it."

"I notice a great deal."

"So have you noticed I am unenthusiastic about you using yourself as bait?" He gave her a grim smile.

"Do you have better ideas? Other than letting me be locked up. That's not an idea."

"Then you'd better observe and hide. Jennifer Belk is driving up the street at this moment."

Kristen swung on her heel to peer down the street, saw the black Escalade, and darted between cars—parked and moving—to reach the cell phone store. She didn't look back or give Nick so much as a wave.

Her message was clear. If he wasn't with her, then he was against her.

As far as he knew, he was the only person nearby who was with her.

THIRTEEN

Kristen hadn't ridden a bicycle in over ten years. After a wobbly start, however, she got her balance and was able to peddle away, certain muscles she'd forgotten about would be sore the next day.

If she lived to see the next day.

But she had talked to US Marshal Callahan himself at Nick's insistence, and he assured her marshals would be in place to keep Kirkpatrick and his men from killing anyone, especially Kristen, or taking anyone else captive. Until Kirkpatrick's men revealed themselves for the violent men they were, Kristen wanted her and Nick to appear as if they were on their own.

So they set out for Nick's family cottage along the shore of Lake Michigan. When they reached their location Kristen intended to send some specific messages to the *Chicago Tribune*, the *Chicago Sun-Times* and the *Milwaukee Journal Sentinel*. If the editors read her

messages, they would soon learn she was challenging the men who had taken her mother. If
they didn't both get killed. And if Kirkpatrick
held up his end of the bargain and released her
mother. If the media was going to say awful
things about her helping the people who had
kidnapped her mother, then Kristen was going
to use them to free her mother.

She hoped.

"Worst-case scenario," she said for the tenth
time, "this doesn't work, as in Kirkpatrick
doesn't take the bait."

"Worst-case scenario is that you get yourself
and your mother killed."

"That too." Kristen fell silent, saving her
breath for riding.

At least she had clean clothes and sneakers
instead of flip-flops and so did Nick. Though
he still needed to shave and her hair needed a
shampoo and vigorous brushing, they would
appear far more respectable when they stopped
to eat.

Which they could also do.

Nick knew the out-of-the-way places, since
they weren't on the main highway. They didn't
want to get caught before the scene was set.

The last call Kristen made was to the kind
family who had helped them to ensure every-

one was all right and tell them where they could find the phone she borrowed.

Kristen frowned. "After that rain, though, I may have to buy her a new one. I'll call tomorrow to make sure."

Nick merely grunted. He wasn't happy with her. He wanted her all locked up safe and sound like a one-of-a-kind jewel—precious and useless in the dark of a hidden compartment. And that made her mad at him. She was tired of being wrapped in cotton wool. She didn't just want to hear about the bad things in the world through her clients and the evening news; she wanted to see it, learn about it in a deep way, so she could work with those who wanted to make changes, bring light into the darkness.

So she endured Nick's grumpy mood and stopped talking altogether. She needed to concentrate on pushing down one pedal after the other again and again, to keep the bike gliding forward. As hard as pedaling was, it beat trying to walk. They traveled much faster. By early evening, she smelled the lake on the breeze. Within an hour, they were cruising along a gravel lane bordered by trees, then emerged into the open with a rustic cabin and the wide, wide blue lake beyond.

"How did your family manage this kind of real estate?" Kristen asked.

"It's been in the family for three generations. We've had enough offers to make us all rich, but we don't want to see the trees cut down and the land turned into another resort hotel." Nick jumped off his bike. "There's a key in a magnetic box under the third rocking chair from the door. Go ahead and go inside while I put these bikes in the shed."

"Thanks." Kristen propped her bike against the railing of a structure too rough-hewn to be called a veranda and too low to be her idea of a porch. A swing and several rocking chairs filled the space beneath the overhanging roof, along with some tables and a pile of children's beach toys.

She counted three chairs from the door and reached beneath. After some fumbling around, she located a little metal box attached to the chair's frame and flipped it open. A key slid into her palm. Eager for shelter where Nick had assured her she could have true privacy, a real bed behind a closed door, she unlocked the front door, stepped inside the cabin—

And came face-to-face with her mother.

Julia Lang sat with her arms and legs bound to the kitchen chair beneath her. Her elegant twist was gone and her hair fell in tangled hanks around her pale face now devoid of makeup. Her suit jacket was torn and the shell beneath grubby. But she held her head erect, her eyes boring into Kristen's as though trying to convey a message she couldn't speak with her mouth duct-taped.

Kristen felt as though an invisible fist had punched her in the middle. She couldn't warn Nick to be careful. She couldn't cry out. She couldn't so much as catch her breath. This was all wrong. Kirkpatrick wasn't supposed to be there yet. But there he was. The creak of a floorboard drew her attention from her mother to the tall, broad-faced man whom she had seen too often in the courtroom.

"You," she squeaked out, and then louder, "You aren't supposed to be here."

"That's right," Kirkpatrick said, "yell so your boyfriend comes running."

"No, Nick, do—"

A hand like a side of beef clamped over her mouth. "That's enough," a familiar voice said in her ear. The voice of the man who had carried her from her car.

She smelled garlic, too much garlic, and gagged.

He removed his hand in a hurry. "Be quiet and I won't tape you up like your ma."

Kristen nodded.

"Now sit down and let's talk," Kirkpatrick said.

Kristen staggered to the chair across from

her mother and dropped onto the wooden seat. "How did you know to come here? The papers were supposed to post that you should call the number I gave to get directions."

"We got our sources." Kirkpatrick grinned.

His only possible source was someone in the Marshals Service.

Nick heard the cry from the house and grinned. She had probably seen a mouse. He should have warned her no one had been at the cabin since Memorial Day and the critters did like to move in uninvited.

He finished locking the bikes in the shed, replaced the key under the overflowing rain barrel and started around the side of the cabin—where he stopped short and dropped to his knees, examining the ground.

The earth was still wet from the storm that morning. It held footprints. Deep footprints. Big footprints. Kristen was a tall girl and not delicately built, but her feet weren't anywhere near this big, nor was she heavy enough to make such a deep impression. She had also not walked along the side of the cabin.

Kristen hadn't seen a mouse; she had seen a criminal. They hadn't spoken to Kirkpatrick yet. The messages giving instructions for Kirkpatrick to find them hadn't gone out long enough ago for him to contact them for directions to the cabin. Only one other person knew Kristen and Nick's location. He could have sent marshals sooner than he said he would, but they weren't supposed to be near the cabin.

But either Kirkpatrick had arrived an hour and a half early, or the marshals were located where they weren't supposed to be. Callahan had sold them out to Kirkpatrick.

Such rage flowed through Nick he could have punched a hole in the log wall beside him. Rage, however, got no one anywhere. He needed to give up his anger toward Michele's father for blaming Nick for her death, for giving him all the terrible jobs he could find in the past year, for suspending him for seeing to Kristen's safety. Callahan wasn't Nick's problem now. He would face his own music afterward. What mattered to Nick was keeping Kristen alive.

First, he needed to reconnoiter and see how many people were in the cabin. He could manage that with little difficulty. He knew every nook and cranny of this house, every creaking board and loose pane of glass.

He returned to the rear of the house and climbed atop the rain barrel. If he slipped off the rim, the splash would give him away. He dug his fingers into the grout between logs and edged his way along the water catcher until he reached a tiny window set high in the wall for ventilation. If he moved from one side to another, he could see the entire great room.

The sight of the judge nearly knocked him off his feet. Seeing Kristen bound to a chair as well set the adrenaline coursing through his veins. She and her mom were helpless. He feared not a single marshal, nor any other law enforcement were on their way for backup. Nick was on his own. One man against the three he counted. More could be hidden in the bathroom or bedrooms.

One inadequately armed man against at least three men with guns and two female hostages.

He slid off the rain barrel, the mud beneath making his descent silent, and edged away from the house. The shed contained firewood and other supplies, some tools. He could wait until dark and cut the electricity. He would know where he was, but they would fumble around. But then, he wouldn't know where they were in relationship to the women. If he smoked them out, the ladies would suffer too, but a little smoke inhalation was far better than a bullet.

Between the woods, the shed and the boathouse, he gathered what he needed. He moved around enough to know no one stood watch outside. No one would shoot into the house, or take more drastic measures, with the judge and her daughter inside. Kirkpatrick and his men counted on their hostages for their security. That surely meant they would keep the ladies alive for the moment anyway.

Alive and unharmed?

Nick yearned to throw himself into that cabin and confront the men. A suicide mission for sure. But if Kristen or her mother were hurt, he would have failed another lady in his life. Another lady who had become so important.

Nerves jumping, he made himself wait the half hour until dusk. Once or twice, from where he waited inside the boathouse, he saw someone look out the front door, hunting for him, he supposed. They didn't venture far from the door. He needed at least one of them to do that. One down would even the odds a little better.

When blowing trees created weird shadows and splashing waves masked other sounds. Then he crept from the boathouse and built a fire on the ground near the corner of the porch. Once it was popping and crackling, looking as though it would reach the porch and set it alight, Nick stretched through the railing and knocked over a table. It fell with a resounding crash.

From inside the cabin, he heard a shout, a protest, then a clear, "Go look."

Just what Nick wanted.

One of Kirkpatrick's men emerged from the cabin and stomped to the fire. When he rounded the corner out of sight of the front windows and door, Nick applied a shovel to the back of his head.

The man crashed to the ground with nearly as much noise as the table. Nick tied him with rope from the shed and dragged him into the crawl space. That done, he added more sticks to the fire, green ones this time, producing billows of sharp smoke.

"Hey, Zivko, what's taking you so—" Boots tramped on the porch and coughing ensued. "What—" he coughed again "—is going—" another cough "—on?"

A demand from inside followed, and the man outside responded, "I can't hardly see out here. Enough smoke the whole place might be on fire. Zivko, where'd you go?"

More commands, more grumbling, more stomping across the porch. Then a bulky shadow appeared in the gloom of evening and greenwood smoke. "Zivko— Ahh!"

This one went down with more grace, folding up like a fan. Nick trussed him up and dragged him beneath the shed built up to avoid being flooded.

Two down, one to go. One armed man to go.

One armed man with two women hostages— important women, the judge because of her position, and Kristen because of what she had come to mean to Nick. He had to lure Kirkpatrick away from the women. The fire had done as much as it could. Nick doused it with a bucket of water he'd set aside for that purpose. Steam and smoke rose into the dusk with the sharp tang of pitch, then died. Nick waited for what happened next, seeking an opportunity to take Kirkpatrick down.

The man had turned out the lights inside, leaving on only the porch light so Nick couldn't see inside. He listened for words or scraping chairs or the click of a cocking gun.

He heard the click first. Then the scrape of a chair. Moments later, footfalls sounded on the pine board floor inside. Two sets of footfalls. Nick's heart squeezed, his gut roiling long before he saw why Kirkpatrick left on the porch light.

He wanted Nick to see him standing behind Kristen with a gun to her head.

"Show yourself, Sandoval, or the daughter goes first, the judge second." Kirkpatrick's voice rang loud and clear.

Nick heard it, though he was already at the back corner of the cabin. The southwest window of the bedroom had a broken lock. Someone always intended to fix it but no one ever got around to it. Nick slid up the sash, glad of the can of WD-40 from the shed supplies making the act silent and smooth. He hefted himself over the sill and landed on the floor like a cat. If he was good at anything, it was walking quietly. As the youngest, being able to sneak around or away from his older siblings had been a matter of survival he practiced to perfection.

He employed the skill now, creeping past the bathroom. At the kitchen island, he crouched, listening.

"You have one minute," Kirkpatrick was saying. "Show yourself or I shoot."

Nick gritted his teeth to stop himself from speaking out loud. *But you need Kristen to learn about your daughter.*

"Tell your friend to come out, Miss Lang," Kirkpatrick persisted.

Kristen remained silent.

"So you don't really care about your ma?" Kirkpatrick's tone held a taunt.

Sweating despite the chills running down his spine, Nick rose from behind the island and snuck forward. When he passed the judge, her eyes grew as round as golf balls. But she didn't make a sound to give him away.

"You have thirty seconds," Kirkpatrick said.

Nick wrapped both hands around the man's gun arm and jerked it down. "And you have zero."

Kirkpatrick swore, fighting for control of his arm and the gun. Nick held on, admiring the older man's strength, his tenacity. A little more pressure, a bit more strength was all Nick needed—Kirkpatrick managed to pull the trigger the instant Nick's pressure on his arm forced him to drop his weapon. Nick kicked it away and the agony in his side dropped him to his knees. "Kristen, help." He looked up.

She slammed her head back, smashing her skull into Kirkpatrick's nose. He howled and drew his hands to his face, blood flowing. Though her hands were still bound, her feet were free. She turned, braced herself against the door frame and kicked Kirkpatrick in the knee, then the belly. He dropped onto the floor, curling up to protect himself from the kicks she applied.

"Rope," Nick gasped. "Back pocket. He won't stay down for long."

She twisted around so she could pull the rope from Nick's pocket and hand it to him. Nick crawled to Kirkpatrick and bound his wrists behind him. The man kicked when Nick reached for his legs, connecting with Nick's wounded side. Blackness swirled before his eyes. Fighting nausea, he managed to get the criminal's ankles bound. Then he must have lost consciousness, for he awoke to find himself lying on the floor with a towel pressed to his wound and Kristen kneeling over him, her face so close to his, her ponytail dangled forward and tickled his face.

He smiled. "You got yourself free."

He had kept her safe. No, God had used him to keep her safe.

"I found scissors in the kitchen." She wiped a cool damp cloth over his face. "And I called an ambulance. You have cell service here."

"Resorts close by." The blackness was taking over again, but he had to do something before he lost consciousness…or worse. "Kristen?"

"I'm here." She touched her lips to his forehead. "You're going to be okay."

"Kristen."

"Don't talk. Save your strength."

"Have to tell you." He forced his eyes open so the last thing he saw was her beautiful blue eyes. "I love you."

Kristen walked into her mother's hospital room to find her father sitting at her bedside holding her hand. Never in her life had Kristen seen her parents show affection to one another.

At her entrance, her father stood and wrapped

his arms around her, holding her tightly against him. A tremble ran through him, and he released a shuddering breath. "I nearly lost both my ladies and I would only have myself to blame."

"Not at all." Kristen drew back and rested her palm against his cheek. "It was Kirkpatrick who was at fault."

"But you came too close to dying. Your mother—" His voice broke and he turned to draw a chair forward for Kristen. "Sit down. We have something to tell you."

"I was going to tell you on our way home Monday," her mother began.

"Tell me what?" Kristen clasped her hands together on her knees, but not too hard. She had several cuts she had gained while cutting the ropes from her wrists.

"I went on a retreat in Switzerland," her father continued the explanation, "because your mother and I had decided to—to end our marriage. We've barely seen or spoken to one another for the past fifteen years."

"I see." Kristen blinked against the tears in her eyes. She didn't know what to say, how her family could get any more distant from one another.

"But this whole experience this week has

shown us how much we still love one another," Mom said with a soft smile for her husband.

"I thought I lost her and you because I wasn't here," he said. "I kept thinking if Julia died, something in me would, and we didn't need to split up to make our lives better. We need to spend more time together."

"And with you too," Mom added. "You're quite a remarkable young woman."

"Even if you did take some foolish risks." Her father's smile took the sting from his words.

Kristen thought the only thing that would make her happier at that moment was to learn that Nick was going to survive the bullet wound to his side. By the time the sheriff and paramedics had reached the cabin, Nick was unconscious, his last words still ringing in Kristen's ears.

I love you.

Surely he hadn't meant it. And yet…

She hugged her arms over her middle. "I look forward to spending more time with both of you. Maybe picnics or boating excursions on the lake? I've gotten kind of fond of the outdoors."

Mom shuddered but nodded. "Whatever you like as long as we get a few art galleries thrown in now and then."

"We'll make good with the time we have,"

Dad said. "The ones we love are too easily snatched away."

"Speaking of loved ones," Mom said, "how is Nick doing?"

Kristen's cheeks grew warm. "I—I don't— Why do you ask?"

"Why don't you go find out how he's doing?" Dad suggested.

Kristen started to rise. "His family is here. I don't want to intrude."

"Intrude," Mom and Dad said together.

The first time she ever knew them to do anything together.

Kristen hugged them both, Mom with care because she had a torn rotator cuff from having her hands tied too harshly behind her, and she was far too thin from lack of food and water. But she would be all right in the end. Better than all right, Kristen realized.

With more confidence than she had known for perhaps her entire life, she returned to the surgical floor to see if anyone would tell her how Nick was doing. At the end of the hall, the waiting room sounded like a party was taking place. She reached the doorway and stood staring at three generations of Sandovals, from probably midsixties to six, all talking at once.

Then Gina spotted her and rushed across the room to hug her. "The hero of the hour."

"I think that's Nick's honor." Kristen pulled back. "All I did was pack his wound with towels."

"And kick Kirkpatrick until he called uncle." Gina grasped her hand. "Let me introduce you to everyone. The folks are dying to meet you."

"Wait." Kristen held back. "Is Nick... Will he be...all right?"

"He hasn't come out of the anesthesia yet, but the surgeon is confident he'll be mostly all right."

Kristen stiffened. "Mostly?"

"The bullet missed any vital organs, but it damaged his hip bone some. He's got a long recovery before him and lots of physical therapy. That's going to make him grumpy. Can you put up with that?"

"After what he put up with from me, I am sure I can."

If he wanted her around and those last words weren't just because he thought he was dying.

"But what about his job? Will he lose it?" she asked. "I mean because he went off the grid with me and all."

"And exposed a crooked marshal." The older man's voice boomed through the room. "They'll give him a medal. It's been all over the news."

"Callahan was arrested a few minutes ago," Gina explained.

"Good. He—" Kristen wasn't able to express her opinion of Callahan. In seconds, everyone surrounded her, asking questions—about her expedition with Nick, about how he brought Kirkpatrick and his men down. Telling the story was easy, as she had already given it to the sheriff and then an FBI agent. She elaborated as much as she could, knowing she was likely to have to give it again to reporters. Just as she finished, a nurse appeared in the doorway.

"Is there a Kristen here?"

The room grew silent, all eyes on her.

"I'm Kristen," she said, heart beginning to race.

"Mr. Sandoval is awake and would like to see you," the nurse said.

Kristen floated to the door, the clan surging behind her.

"Just Kristen right now," the nurse said.

"But I'm his mother," Mrs. Sandoval protested.

"Girlfriends come first, Nancy," her husband reminded her.

"But I'm not—"

Her protest ignored, Kristen was swept down

the corridor to a dimly lit room where Nick lay beneath a sheet, his face as pale as the linen. But his lips and eyes smiled at her, and he reached one hand toward her. "Kristen."

She took his hand in both of hers. "Hey, Nick. You look terrible."

"That's the nicest thing anyone's ever said to me."

They fell silent, their eyes locked until Kristen drew the courage to ask, "Do you remember what you said before you passed out?"

"Of course I do. I asked for a pizza."

She laughed. "That's right. With pepperoni."

"I was delirious. I prefer sausage." He raised her hand to his cheek. "I'll have to be careful how much pizza I eat, especially nice thick Chicago-style, if I'm going to be laid up for weeks. Can you put up with me?"

"Yes."

"Will you?"

"Yes."

"I'll probably end up with a boring desk job, you know."

"You could never be boring, no matter what your job."

"Wow, you talk like you might like me a little."

"I like you a lot." She leaned down and kissed him. "In fact, I love you."

"And I love you," he said.

And they kissed again, to seal a future of love and laughter and their two families.

EPILOGUE

No wonder brides still insisted on long gowns. The skirts hid knocking knees. Her father's hand over hers in the crook of his elbow masked how Kristen's fingers shook. No one could see the migration of butterflies swarming through her middle, but she knew they were there—butterflies that managed to feel like half horses, wings fluttering and hooves galloping around and around as though they were butterfly ponies on a carousel.

Butterponies? Horseflies? No, horseflies were already a large, biting insect. Maybe flutterhorses.

Kristen giggled at her own nonsense thoughts. Her father smiled down at her and squeezed her hand. In the back row of the church, eight of Nick's male cousins, ages between fifteen and twenty, glanced her way and grinned.

Kristen winked at the youngest and cutest

one. He blushed and ducked his head, his hair falling over his forehead.

Nick must have looked that way in his teens—unruly hair, gangly body and a grin that would have ladies following him around.

If she and Nick were blessed enough to have a son, he would look like that—she hoped. She wanted all their sons to resemble their father, and their daughters to favor Kristen or the women in Nick's family. At least two sons and two daughters. A big family like Nick's.

Thoughts of bearing Nick's children made Kristen's ears and cheeks turn so hot they must resemble the red roses in her bouquet. Red for warmth. Red for joy. Red for love. On this frosty November afternoon, the attendants wore red velvet dresses and carried white roses.

The last of those attendants, the matron of honor, Nick's sister Gina, approached the front of the church. The music changed, began to modulate, to swell into the bride's processional, and Kristen's flutterhorses returned, beating double time to the throb of the organ. Gina reached the line of bridesmaids, six to accommodate the women her mother insisted she must ask, six more than Kristen and Nick wanted.

My daughter just gets married once, Mother had insisted. *You'll do it right.*

"Right" seemed to involve inviting everyone in both extended families as well as everyone who worked in the courthouse, or so it seemed. As Nick moved to the head of the aisle and the sanctuary suddenly appeared a mile long, her beloved, the man who could banish her flutter-horses and melt her heart with the mere touch of his hand on hers, waited for her too far away. He would change his mind before she got there. She would trip over the scalloped lace hem of her dress and fall, thus never reaching him. A siren would scream past on the highway and wake her up to realize the past six months had been the best dream of her life.

Tears filled her eyes. She raised her lids, conscious she must not blink and send the drops running through her carefully applied makeup.

Yes, she wore makeup—mascara heavy on her lashes, foundation, powder, blush, bronzer and who knew what else on her nose and cheeks. It was so stiff she feared she would crack the mask if she smiled too much.

It was so stiff she knew everything was not a dream—makeup, gown, a church full of people. This was her day. Hers and Nick's. Who cared if she smiled and flawed the layers of cosmetics? She was smiling at Nick waiting for her at the altar.

Kristen took a step forward.

"Wait for your father to go first." The wedding planner slipped behind Kristen and fluffed out her train. "Remember how I showed you to walk."

She didn't remember. She didn't care if she remembered. She wasn't there to impress anyone with the gracefulness she knew she didn't possess. Her only purpose in that room at that moment was to get to Nick as fast as she could and become his wife.

Only the wedding planner's grip on her elbow stopped Kristen from releasing her father's arm and racing down the aisle and into Nick's arms.

The music reached its crescendo. Everyone in the audience rose and turned toward the aisle, turned to stare at Kristen.

She was going to be sick. She was going to crumple into a heap on the white vinyl crash lining the walkway and begin to blubber like a baby.

The crash. A good name for what was going to happen to her.

A sharp movement at the front of the sanctuary caught Kristen's attention. Nick had raised one hand as though beckoning her forward. Beckoning her to his side.

Kristen took a deep breath and stepped forward. The guests faded into a blur no more significant than houses on an unfamiliar street. With her gaze on the man awaiting her at the altar, Kristen found her footsteps steady, even, purposeful. The endless-seeming aisle slipped away, and she was suddenly at Nick's side, his hand gripping hers, so warm, so firm.

"Dearly beloved," the pastor said.

And the most important part of the ceremony began. Words of wisdom from the pastor, Nick's voice full of conviction speaking his vows, her own far clearer than she thought she could manage in front of five hundred people. Then Nick kissed her, his "I love you," nearly drowned out in the round of applause.

Nick and Kristen led the way back down the aisle to receive congratulations and hugs from dozens of relatives. Most important of those were Kristen's own parents, who were heading off on a monthlong cruise for a second honeymoon, their marriage renewed. Nick's parents and siblings welcomed her like another daughter and sister, more love than she ever thought she would have. Kristen knew life wouldn't always be smooth, but with Nick at her side and the two of them surrounded by family, certainty ran to her core that she would never have to face the bumps and mountains along life's journey alone.

* * * * *

If you enjoyed Lethal Ransom,
*look for this other Love Inspired Suspense
title by Laurie Alice Eakes.*

Perilous Christmas Reunion

*Find more great reads at
www.LoveInspired.com*

Dear Reader,

Thank you for reading *Lethal Ransom*. This idea has been in my head a long time, and I am grateful to be able to write it and share it with you all.

Kristen is the kind of heroine I can relate to—caring about others, smart and courageous. Yet she doesn't think she has strengths and abilities to survive. Nick is haunted by events in his past that rattled his self-confidence. As they fight for their very lives, they learn they work better together than separately, bringing out the best in themselves and one another.

Once again, I have made my beloved Midwest the setting. Crowded city streets and vast woods create so many lovely opportunities for danger and intrigue.

I love to hear from my readers. You can contact me through my website http://www.lauriealiceeakes.com or find me on Twitter @ LaurieAEakes or Facebook.com/AuthorLaurie-AliceEakes/

Laurie Alice Eakes

Get 4 FREE REWARDS!

We'll send you 2 FREE Books plus 2 FREE Mystery Gifts.

Love Inspired® books feature contemporary inspirational romances with Christian characters facing the challenges of life and love.

FREE
Value Over
$20
